**"SNOWS-OF-SALVATION . . .
SNOWS-OF-SALVATION
COME IN PLEASE. . . ."**

"Who is that? Get the hell off this freq', there's a mixed-load dockin' in progress here! Do you–"

"This is the ship your navy attacked . . . the ship from outside."

First there was silence, then: "What is it you want here?"

"We want one thousand tons of processed hydrogen, sent out on the trajectory I give you. If you fail to do this, I'll destroy your distillery and you'll all die."

"You won't destroy us. Even the Demarchy would want you dead if you did that."

"We're not from your system; you're nothing to us. The Demarchy is nothing. I hope you all go to hell together for what you've done to us; but Snows-of-Salvation will get there first unless you obey my orders. You have twenty-five thousand seconds to give us the hydrogen or be destroyed . . . !"

THE OUTCASTS OF HEAVEN BELT

by

JOAN D. VINGE

A SIGNET BOOK
NEW AMERICAN LIBRARY
TIMES MIRROR

To our parents, all four of them

NAL BOOKS ARE AVAILABLE AT QUANTITY DISCOUNTS WHEN USED TO PROMOTE PRODUCTS OR SERVICES. FOR INFORMATION PLEASE WRITE TO PREMIUM MARKETING DIVISION, THE NEW AMERICAN LIBRARY, INC., 1633 BROADWAY, NEW YORK, NEW YORK 10019.

This book was serialized in slightly different form in *Analog* magazine

SIGNET TRADEMARK REG. U.S. PAT. OFF. AND FOREIGN COUNTRIES
REGISTERED TRADEMARK—MARCA REGISTRADA
HECHO EN CHICAGO, U.S.A.

SIGNET, SIGNET CLASSICS, MENTOR, PLUME, MERIDIAN AND NAL BOOKS *are published by The New American Library, Inc., 1633 Broadway, New York, New York 10019*

FIRST SIGNET PRINTING, DECEMBER, 1978

4 5 6 7 8 9 10 11 12 13

PRINTED IN THE UNITED STATES OF AMERICA

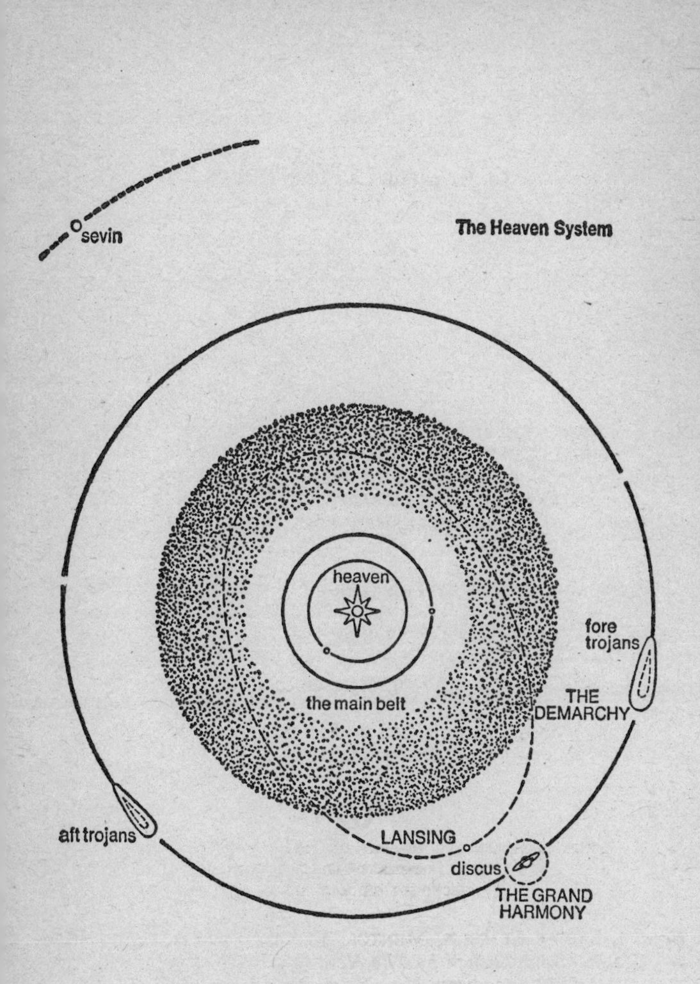
The Heaven System
sevin
heaven
the main belt
fore
trojans
THE
DEMARCHY
aft trojans
LANSING
discus
THE GRAND
HARMONY

Two are better than one; because they have
a good reward for their labours. For if
they fall, the one will lift up his fellow:
but woe to him that is alone when he falleth;
for he hath not another to help him up.

—Ecclesiastes

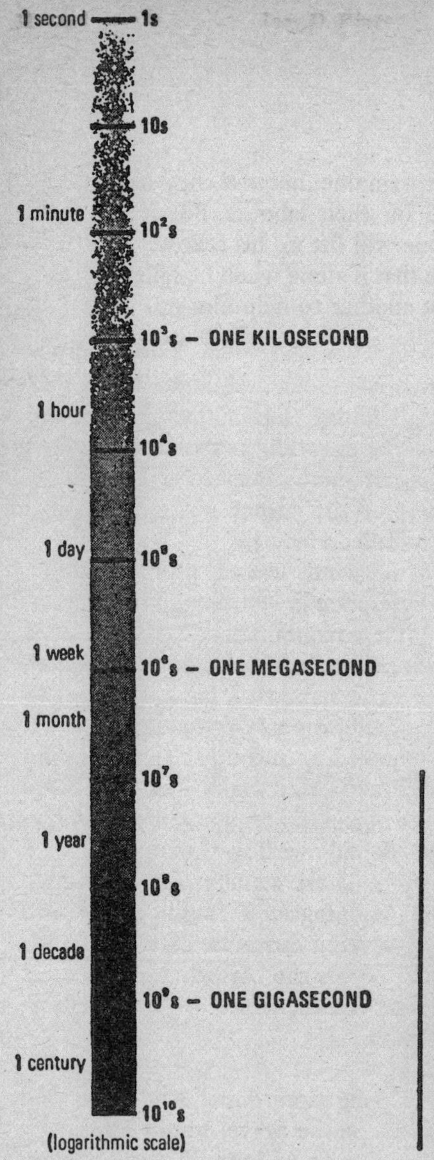

ONE HOUR– approximately three kiloseconds

ONE DAY– approximately eighty kiloseconds

TWO WEEKS– slightly more than one megasecond

ONE YEAR– approximately thirty megaseconds

THIRTY YEARS– approximately one gigasecond

There are more stars in the galaxy than there are droplets of water in the Boreal Sea. Only a fraction of those stars wink and glitter, like snowflakes passing through the light, in the unending night sky above the darkside ice. And out of those thousand thousand visible stars, the people of the planet Morningside had made a wish on one—called Heaven.

Sometimes when the winds ceased, a brittle silence would settle over the darkside ice sheet; and it might seem to a Morningside astronomer, in the solitude of his observatory, that all barriers had broken down between his planet and the stars, that the very hand of interstellar space brushed his pulse. Space lapped at his doorway, the night flowed up and up and up, merging imperceptibly with the greater night that swallowed all mornings, and all Morningsides, and all the myriad stars whose numbers would overflow the sea.

And he would think of the starship *Ranger*, which had gone up from Morningside's fragile island into that endless night: a silvered dustmote carried on a violent invisible breeze across the cathedral distances of space, drawn from candleflame to candleflame through the darkness....

They would be a long time gone. And what had seemed to the crew to be the brave, bright immensity of their fusion craft shrank to insignificance as they left the homeworld further and further behind—as the *Ranger* became only one more mote, lost among countless unseen motes in the fathomless depths of night. But like an ember within a tinderbox, their lives gave the ship its own warm heart of light, and life. The days passed, and the months, and years . . . and light-years, while seven men and women watched over the ship's needs, and one another's. Their shared past patterned their present with images of the world they had left behind, visions of the future they hoped to bring back to it. They were bound for Heaven, and like true believers they found that belief instilled a deeper meaning in the charting of stars and the tending of hydroponic vats, in their silence and their laughter, in every song and memory they carried with them from home.

And at last one star began to separate from all the rest, centering on the ship's viewscreen, becoming a focus for their combined hope. Years had dwindled to months and finally weeks, as, decelerating now, backing down from near the speed of light, they kept their rendezvous with the new system. They passed the orbit of Sevin, the outermost of Heaven's worlds, where the new sun was still scarcely more than an ice-crowned point of light. Counting the days now, like children reaching toward Christmas, the crew anticipated journey's end before them: all the riches and wonders of the Heaven Belt.

But before they reached their final destination, they would encounter one more wonder that was no creation of humankind—the gas giant Discus, a billowing ruby set in a plate of silver rings. They watched it expand until it obliterated more of this black and alien sky than the face of their own sun had blocked in the dusty sky of home. They closed with the giant's lumbering course, slipping past like a cautious firefly. And while the crew sat together in the dayroom, gazing out in awe at its splendor, the captain and the navigator discovered something new, something quite unexpected, on the ship's displays: four unknown ships, powered by antiquated chemical rockets, on an intercepting course. . . .

RANGER (DISCAN SPACE) + 0 SECONDS

"Pappy, are they still closing?"

"Still closing, Betha." Clewell Welkin bent forward as new readings appeared at the bottom of the screen. "But the rate's holding steady. They must be cutting power; they couldn't do ten gees forever. Christ, don't let them hit us again. . . ."

Betha struck the intercom button again with her fist, "It's going to be all right. No one else will get near us." Her voice shook, someone else's voice, not Betha Torgussen's, and no one answered, "Come on, somebody, answer me. Eric! Eric! Switch on–"

"Betha." Clewell leaned out across the padded seat arm, caught her shoulder.

"Pappy, they don't answer."

"Betha, one of those ships, it's not falling back! It's–"

She brushed away his hand, searching the readouts on the screen. "Look at it! They want to *take* us. They must; it's burning chemical fuel, and they can't afford to waste that much." She held her breath, knuckles whitening on the cold metal panel. "They're getting too close. Show them our tail, Pappy."

Pale eyes flickered in his seamed face. "Are you–?"

She half-rose, pushed back from the panel, down into the seat again. "Clewell, they tried to kill us! They're armed, they want to take our ship and they will, and that's the only way to stop them. . . . Let them cross our tail, Navigator."

"Yes, Captain." He turned away from her toward the panel, and began to punch in the course change that would end their pursuit.

At the final moment Betha switched the screen from simulation to outside scan, picked out the amber fleck of the pursuing ship thirty kilometers behind them—watched it fleetingly made golden by the alchemy of supercharged particles from her ship's exhaust. And watched its gold darken again into the greater darkness shot with stars. She shuddered, not feeling it, and cut power.

"What—what do we do now?" Clewell drifted up off the seat, against the restraining belt, as the ship's acceleration ceased. The white fringe of his hair stood out from his head like frost.

Before her on the screen the rings of Discus edged into view, eclipsing the night: the plate of striated silver, twenty separate bands of utter blackness and moon-white, the setting for the rippling red jewel of gas that was the central planet. Her hand was on the selector dial, her eyes burned with the brightness, paralyzing her will. She shut her eyes, and turned the dial.

The intercom was broken. They still sat at the table, Eric and Sean and Nikolai, Lara and Claire; they looked up at her, laughing, breathing again, looked out through the dome at the glory of Discus on the empty night . . . . She opened her eyes. And saw empty night. *Oh, God,* she thought. The room was empty; they were gone. *Oh, God.* Only stars, gaping beyond the shattered plastic of the dome, crowding the blackness that had swallowed them all. . . . She didn't scream, lost in the soundless void.

"They're all—gone. All of them. That warhead . . . it shattered the dome."

She turned to see Clewell, his face bloodless and empty; saw their lives, with everything suddenly gone. Thinking, frightened, *He looks so old. . . .* She released her seatbelt mindlessly, pushed herself along the panel to his side and took his hands. They held each other close, in silence.

A squirming softness batted against her head; she jerked upright as claws like tiny needles caught a foothold in the flesh of her shoulder. "Rusty!" She reached up to pull the cat loose, began to drift and hooked a foot under the rung along the panel base. Golden eyes peered at her from a round brindled face, above a nose half black and half orange; mottled whiskers twitched as the mouth formed a *meow?* like an unoiled gate hinge. Betha's hands tightened over an urge to fling the cat across the room. *What right does an animal have to be alive, when five human beings are dead?* She turned her face away as Rusty stretched a patchwork paw to touch her, *mrr*ing consolation for an imcomprehensible grief. Betha cradled her, kissed the furred forehead, comforted by the soft knot of her warmth.

Clewell caught Rusty's drifting tail, bloodied at the tip. "She barely got out."

Betha nodded.

"Why did we ever come to Heaven?" His voice shook.

She looked up. "You know why we came!" She stopped, forcing control. "I don't know . . . I mean . . . I mean, I thought I knew . . ." Four years ago, as they left Morningside, she had been sure of everything: her destination, her happiness, her marriage, her life. And now, suddenly, incredibly, only life remained. *Why?*

Because the people of Morningside, the bleak innermost world of a pitiless red dwarf star, had a dream of Heaven. Heaven: A G-type sun system without an

Earthlike planet, but with an asteroid belt rich in accessible metals. And with Discus, a gas giant ringed in littered splendor by frozen water, methane, and ammonia—the elemental keys to life. The ore-rich Belt and the frozen gases had made it feasible—almost easy—to build up a colony entirely self-sufficient in its richness; heaven in every sense of the word to colonists from Sol's asteroid belt, who had always been dependent on Earth for basic survival needs. And it had become a dream for another colony, Morningside, hungry now for something more than survival: the dream that they could establish contact with the Heaven Belt, and negotiate a share in its overflowing bounty.

The dream that had carried the starship *Ranger* across three light-years; that had been shattered with the shattered dayroom, by the reality of sudden death. The desolation burned again across her eyes; her mind saw the *Ranger's* one-hundred-meter spindle form, every line as familiar as her own face, every centimeter blueprinted on her memory . . . saw it flawed by one tiny, terrible wound; saw five faces, lost to her now in darkness, endlessly falling. . . .

Clewell said softly, "What now?"

"We go on—go on as planned."

"You want to go on trying to make contact with "Do you want to lead them home by the hand, to these . . ." His hand pointed at the ruin on the screen. murder all of Morningside? Isn't it enough—"

Betha shook her head, clinging to the arms of her seat. "We don't have any choice! You know that. We don't have enough hydrogen on board to get the ship back to ramscoop speeds. We have to refuel somewhere in Heaven, or we'll never get home." A vision of home stunned her: firelight on dark beams, on the night before their departure—a little boy's face bright with tears, buried against her shirt. *Mommy . . . I dreamed you had to die to go to Heaven.* Remembering her child's sobs waking out of nightmare, her own eyes filled with tears and the endless darkness. She bit her lip. *Goddamn it, I'm not a child, I'm thirty-five years old!*

"Pappy, don't start acting like an old man." She frowned, and watched his irritation strip ten years from his face. Without looking, she reached out to blank the viewscreen. "We don't have any choice now. We have to go on with it." *We have to pay them back*, her eyes flickered, hard edges of sapphire glinting. She tossed Rusty carefully away, watched her cat-paddle uselessly as she drifted out into the room. "We have enough fuel left to get us around the system . . . but who do we trust? Why did they attack us? And those ships, chemical rockets—they shouldn't have anything like that outside of a museum! It doesn't make sense."

"Maybe they were pirates, renegades. There's nothing else that fits." Clewell's hand hung in the air, uncertain.

"Maybe." She sighed, knowing that renegades had no place in Heaven. Having no choice except to believe it, she forgot that the angry, mindless face that had cursed her on their screen had called her *pirate*. "We'll go on in to the main Belt, to the capital at Lansing, as planned, then. And then . . . we'll find a way to get what we need."

TOLEDO PLANETOID (DEMARCHY SPACE)
+ 30 KILOSECONDS

Wadie Abdhiamal, negotiator for the Demarchy, stirred sluggishly, dragged up out of sleep by the chiming of the telephone. He turned the lights up enough to make out its form and switched it on. "Yes?" He saw Lije MacWong's mahogany face brighten on the screen, pushed himself up on an elbow in the bed.

"Sorry to wake you up, Wadie."

He grinned. "I'll bet you are." MacWong enjoyed getting up early. Wadie glanced at the digital clock in the phone's base. "Somebody need a negotiator at this time of night? Don't the people ever sleep?"

"I hope they're all sleepin' now. . . . Are you alone?"

Wadie glanced back over his shoulder at Kimoru's brown, sleek side, her tumbled black hair. She sighed in her sleep. He looked back at MacWong's image, judged from the disapproval in the pale-blue eyes that MacWong already knew the answer. Annoyed but not showing it, he said, "No, I'm not."

"Pick up the receiver."

Wadie obeyed, cutting off sound from the general speaker. He listened, silent, for the few seconds more it took MacWong to surprise him out of his sleep-fog. "Be down as soon as I can."

He got out of bed, half-drifting in the scant gravity, and went into the bathroom to wash and shave.

When he returned he found Kimoru sitting up in bed, the pinioned comforter pulled up to her chin. She blinked reproachfully, her eyelids showing lavender.

"Wadie, darlin' "—a hint of spite—"it's not even morning! Whyever are you gettin' up already; am I such a bore in bed?" A hint of desperation.

"Kimoru." He moved across the comfortable confinement of the room to kiss her lingeringly. "That's a hell of a thing to say to me. Duty called, I've got to leave . . . you know I hate to get up early. Particularly when you're here. Get your beauty sleep; I'll come back to take you out to breakfast—or lunch, if you prefer." He fastened his shirt with one hand, touched her cheek with the other.

"Well, all right." She slithered down under the cover. "But don't be too late. You know I've got to charm a customer for dear old Chang and Company at fifty kilosecs." She yawned. Her teeth were very bright, and sharp. "I don't know why you don't get a decent job. Only a government man would put up with a schedule like yours . . . or have to."

Or a geisha—? He went on dressing, didn't say it out loud; knowing that she didn't have a choice, and that to remind her of it was unnecessary and tactless. A woman who had been sterilized for genetic defects had very few opportunities open to her, in a society that saw a woman as a potential mother above all else. If she was married to an understanding husband, one who was willing to let a contract mother provide him with heirs, she could continue to lead a normal life. But a woman divorced for sterility—or an unmarried sterile woman—had only two alternatives: to work at a menial, unpleasant job, exposed to radiation from the dirty postwar atomic batteries; or to work as a geisha, entertaining the clients of a corporation. It was prostitution; but it was accepted. A geisha had few rights and little prestige, but she did have security, comfortable surroundings, fine clothes, and enough money to support her when she passed her prime. It was a sterile existence, but physical sterility left her with little choice.

Knowing the alternatives, Wadie neither blamed nor censured. And it struck him frequently that in working for the government, he had picked a career that most people respected less than formal prostitution—and one that had left his private life as barren of real relationships as any geisha's. He looked past his own reflection in the mirror, at Kimoru, already asleep again with one slender arm reaching out toward the empty half of the bed. He had no children, no wife. Most of the women he saw socially were women like Kimoru, geishas he met while negotiating disputes for the corporations that used them. He avoided them while he was on assignment, because he avoided anything that could remotely be considered a bribe. But in their free time the geishas liked to choose their own escort, and he had enough money to show them a good time.

But he rarely stayed in one place long enough to get to know any woman well; and the few normal women he had known at all had bored him with their endless insipid conversation, their endless coquetry.

Wadie brushed back his dark curling hair and settled the soft beret carefully on his head. He was a fastidious dresser, even at dawn. It was expected. He picked up a silver ring set with rubies, slipped it onto his thumb. It had been a gift of gratitude, from two people he had helped long megaseconds before, a husband-and-wife prospecting team. He remembered that woman again—a woman pilot, a sound, healthy woman who had chosen to be sterilized in order to go into space. No kind of woman at all, really; because no real woman would willingly reject a home and family. That woman had been a freak—stubborn, defensive, self-righteous; a woman out of her place, out of her depth. And yet her partner had married her. But he had been a kind of freak himself; a mediaman—a professional liar—with scruples. It was no wonder the two of them chose to spend the rest of their lives in the middle of nowhere, picking over salvage on ruined worlds. . . .

Wadie shook his head at the memory, looking into the mirror, into the past. He wondered again, as he had wondered before, what bizarre chemistry had drawn them together, and still kept them together. And wondered briefly, almost enviously, why that chemistry had never worked on him. He shrugged on his loose forest-green jacket, buttoned the high collar above the embroidered silken geometries. Hell, he was eleven hundred and fifty megaseconds old—thirty-eight Old World years—most of them spent solving everyone else's problems, living everyone else's life instead of his own. If he hadn't found a woman by now who would accept him on his own terms, or one who could make him forget everything else, he never would. He wasn't getting any younger; if he wanted a child, he couldn't afford to wait much longer. When he finished this new assignment he would hire a contract mother to bear his child and raise it while he was away. He glanced back one last time at sleeping Kimoru as he left the apartment, closing the door quietly.

* * *

Wadie yawned discreetly as he left the building's shadow and started across the quiet square. It was barely daylight now; the glow of the fluorescent lamps brightened like dawn in the ceiling's imitation sky, ten meters above his head. The magnetized soles of his polished boots clicked faintly on the polished metal of the square, added security in the slight spin-gravity of Toledo planetoid. The surface of the square curved along the inside hull of a massive, hollowed chunk of iron, a rich miner's harvest and a solid home, but one that was beginning, ungraciously, to show its age. The silvery geometric filigree of pure mineral iron beneath his feet had been preserved once by a thin bonding film, but it was oxidizing now as the film wore away. He could trace rusty paths, dull reddish brown in the early light, leading his eyes across the square and under the tarnished rococo wall to the entrance of the government center. Symptoms of a deeper illness . . . something like panic choked him; from habit he took a long breath, and eased back from the edge, from admitting that the disease would be terminal. He went on toward the center, ordering the lace at his cuffs. *Living well is the best defense*, he thought sourly.

Lije MacWong was waiting for him inside. Officially Wadie worked for the citizens of the Demarchy; actually he worked for MacWong. MacWong, the People's Choice: the Demarchy's absolute democracy was an unpredictable water beneath the fragile ship of government, and it had drowned countless unwary representatives. But MacWong moved instinctively with the flow of popular opinion, sometimes even risked diverting that flow to suit his own vision of the people's needs. He did the people's business, and made them like it. Wadie wondered from time to time what MacWong's secret was; and wondered whether he really wanted to know. "Peace 'n' prosperity, Lije."

MacWong glanced up as Wadie entered the office, ice-blue eyes placid in his dark face. "Peace 'n' prosperity, Wadie." He rose, returned a formal bow, and moved reluctantly away from his aquarium.

Wadie peered past him for a glimpse of the fish—

three glittering golden things no larger than a finger, with tails of shining gossamer, moving sinuously through sea grasses in the green-lit water. The goldfish were the only nonhuman creatures he had ever seen, and for all he knew MacWong was still paying for them. He pulled off his hat, watched its soft mushroom roundness begin to flatten beside MacWong's on the desk top. "With all due respect, I trust this news about a Mysterious Message from Outer Space is genuine, an' I'm not here because you like to see me suffer." He sank slowly into MacWong's neocolonial desk chair, smoothed wrinkles from his jacket.

"Have a seat." MacWong smiled tolerantly. "The 'message' is genuine. These aren't home movies I'm goin' to show you." He leaned carefully against the corner of his desk, avoiding the fresco of silver animal heads, and flicked a switch on the communications inset. Nothing happened. "Dammit." He picked up a platinum paperweight shaped like a springing cat and dropped it on the panel. The impact was unimpressive, but the Kleinfelter mural projection on the far wall faded, and was replaced by the image of a woman's face. "I don't know what I'll do if this desk quits working. They don't build 'em like they used to." He set the paperweight gently back in place.

"They don't build 'em at all, Lije." Wadie traced the scrolled embroidery on his jacket front; his fingers froze as he looked up at the screen. "A hologram? Where'd you get that, MacWong?"

"We picked it out of the air, or space, anyhow, thirty kilosecs ago. It's a genuine hologramic transmission; it took us ten kilosecs to figure that out. And it's not beamed. Think of the power and bandwidth something like that requires! I don't know anybody who can do that for the hell of it any more."

"Not many that can do it at all—" He broke off,

watching, listening, as the woman's voice rose. Her skin was pale to the point of colorlessness, like her cropped, floating hair; her face was long and angular. She wore a faded shirt open at the neck, without jewelry. In her thirties, he judged, and making no attempt to cover it up; her plainness was almost painful. He put it out of his mind, concentrating on her voice. She spoke Anglo, but with an unfamiliar accent; the most common words seemed to take on extra syllables in her mouth.

". . . please identify yourselves further. We were not aware of violating your space. We are not, repeat *not*, from your system; and we—" She was interrupted by a noise that barely recorded; Wadie saw her pale skin blush with anger, her eyes sharpen like cut sapphire. He glanced at MacWong.

"The Ringer navy," MacWong said. "Their 'cast went the other way. This is all we picked up."

The woman glanced offscreen, and spoke words that he couldn't hear, insulting words, he guessed; but her voice was steady as she faced the screen again. "This is not a Belter ship, we are not 'Demarchists,' and we have committed no acts of 'piracy.' You have no authority over my ship; permission to board is denied. But if you will give us co-ords for your—"

Again she was interrupted; he watched tension grow, tightening her face. "We're not armed—" And resolution: "But we deny your 'right of seizure.' Pappy, get us—" She turned away again, and her image was ripped apart by a burst of red static. For half a second more he saw her, and then the screen went white.

"Well?"

Wadie loosened his hands on the metal frame of the chair. "Did they destroy it? Is that all?"

MacWong shook his head. "The ship took a hit, but it got away from the Ringers—all but one of 'em. We monitored some of their followups; that alien ship is a ramscoop, and when one of the Ringer pursuit craft got too close she just used the exhaust to melt it into scrap. Maybe that indignant Viking Queen isn't armed, but she's dangerous."

Wadie said nothing, waiting.

"We don't know where the ship is now, or even why it's here. But I have some ideas. She said it was from outside the system, and I believe that. Nobody in the Belt has anything that sophisticated any more. And a woman runnin' it—particularly a woman who looks like that—"

"Maybe she's an albino . . . maybe she's from the Main Belt. The scavengers don't care who goes into space; they've got no protection against radiation anyhow. Maybe they got very lucky on salvage." And yet he knew that MacWong was right; that the woman and her accent were too alien.

MacWong looked at him. "Nobody gets that lucky. What's wrong, Wadie, the miracle too much for you? This isn't some mediaman's fantasy, believe me. That's a ship from Outside, the first contact we've had with the rest of humanity in over three gigasecs. And the course they set away from the Rings could be taking them to the old capital, Lansing. If that's right, there can only be one reason why that ship is here: they don't know about the Civil War. They've come to Heaven lookin' for golden streets, and when they learn there aren't any left we'll never see 'em again. We can't let that happen. . . ."

"What good would one ship do us now?" He stared at the blank wall screen, against his will felt another question stubbornly taking form.

"*That* ship could do us all the good in the universe." MacWong picked up his platinum cat. "*That* ship is treasure, that ship is power . . . that ship could save us."

Wadie nodded, admitting to himself that the ship's immense fusion reactor alone could give the Demarchy the start to rebuild capital industry. And God only knew what other technology—functioning technology—they might have on board. Just the possession of a ship like that would change the Demarchy's snow dealings with the Rings forever. They could even bypass Discus and the Ringers, set up distilleries of their own out on Sevin's moons. . . .

For as long as he could remember he had lived with signs of a society gradually coming apart at the seams, alone in the wasteland that civil war had made of Heaven Belt. Because of its peripheral location, the Demarchy had survived the Civil War relatively intact. But the Main Belt had been destroyed, and now the Demarchy's only outside trade contact was with the Grand Harmony of the Discan Rings, and the Ringers were barely surviving. The Demarchy was slipping down with it, but because it had so much further to go, he had discovered that no one else seemed to realize the truth. They were blinded by the fierce, traditional self-interest that was the Demarchy's strength—and perhaps, now, its fatal weakness.

He had become a negotiator, hoping to bind up his people's self-inflicted wounds. He had believed that somehow the unifying element, the common bond of need that joined every human being, could be used as a force against disintegration and decay; that the Demarchy would continue, that they would find an answer. And with this ship . . . His imagination leaped, fell back as the question struck him down: Who would control a ship like that . . . and who could control the ones who did control it? "But as you said, that ship will go back home, once they see what's left of Lansing."

"Maybe." MacWong flicked dust off of his cuff. "But Osuna thinks they might need to refuel first. It's a long way home to anywhere from here. They're not likely to go back to the Rings to get fuel, under the circumstances. Which means they might come to us; if they need processed hydrogen, there's no place else to go. So I'm sendin' out everyone I can spare. I want you at Mecca. The distilleries will make it a prime target, and you're more experienced at dealing with—'aliens'—than anybody on the staff."

Wadie accepted the tacit compliment, the tacit distaste, remembered fifty million seconds spent in the Grand Harmony of the Discan Rings, and things it had shown him that he had never expected to see. He stood up, reaching for his hat. "What if they're not in the mood for negotiation?"

"I don't expect they will be. But that doesn't matter; you're paid to put them in the mood. Promise them anythin', but keep them here, stall that ship, until we can take control of it."

Wadie adjusted his beret, looked back from the mirroring wall. "What do you mean by 'we,' Lije? Just who *is* goin' to control that ship? It won't be the government, the people will see to that. And the first kid on the rock to own one—"

MacWong was not amused. "I sometimes wonder if you didn't spend too much time with the Ringers, Abdhiamal. Dammit, Wadie, I'm not still questioning your loyalty, after two hundred megasecs. But there are still some who do; who think maybe you'd really like to see a centralized government here." He stopped. "There'll be a general meeting to settle the issue once we have the ship." He leaned forward across the gargoyled desk. "The Demarchy has to have that ship, an' no one but the Demarchy."

"You're the boss." Wadie bowed.

"No." MacWong straightened. "The Demarchy is the boss. We give the people what they think they want. Nothing else means anything. Forget that, and we're out of a job—or worse. If I was you, I wouldn't ever forget it."

And knowing that MacWong never did, Wadie left the office.

RANGER (IN TRANSIT, DISCUS TO LANSING) + 130 KILOSECONDS

Betha left the hydroponics lab at last, began to climb up through the hollow silence of the central stairwell. She could no longer remember how many times she had climbed these stairs in the past two days; the duties of a crew of seven were an endless treadmill of labor for a crew of two. She passed the machine shop on the fourth level, kept on, reached their sleeping quarters on the third. One more level above, across the well, the flashing red light over the sealed dayroom door caught her unwilling eyes. She stopped, wrenched out of her fatigue by a fresh rush of grief.

She stepped hurriedly through to the corridor that ringed the stairwell on the third level, that gave access to seven private rooms . . . and all that remained of five human beings who were lost to her forever. To her right, Lara's room; everything in its place, mirroring the precision of Lara's mind. . . . Betha remembered the crisp directness of her voice across an examining table in the ship's infirmary; her graying hair, the warm concern in her gray eyes that denied her clinical detachment. There was a padded stool in Lara's room made from a cetoid vertebra; a *Color Atlas of the Diseases of Fish, Amphibians, and Reptiles.* She had been a medical researcher on Morningside, before their family had become a crew and she had become their doctor; but marine biology had been her hobby, her real love. And Sean, the smartass, had written a song, "Lara and the Leviathan," that swallowed her up in verses about this "cetoid monster," the *Ranger*. . . .

Through the open doorway directly before her, Betha could see a tangle of electronics gear, Nikolai's balalaika laid out on the sleeping bag on the platform of his bed. She pictured him, balding, bearded, brooding; with a voice like an echo escaping from a well. . . . A patient, skillful teacher, an electronics expert—a repairman, at home, serving the entire Borealis moiety. She remembered him laughing, dodging the shoe she had thrown at Sean for calling her *Ranger* a whale. . . .

She turned to her left, moved along the curving hallway against the currents of memory, like a woman wading into the sea. . . . Remembering Claire, placidly moon-faced, curly-haired; plump, fair farmer's daughter . . . Sean, the red-haired kid among them, only twenty-four . . .

Betha hesitated, finding herself before her own doorway. She glanced in, at her cluttered desk, her rumpled bedding. She moved on desperately, as though she would drown herself, to the next room . . . to Eric. Eric van Helsing, social scientist, moiety ombudsman, spokesman. . . .

> You are the rain, my love, sweet water
> Flowing through the desert of my life.

The words of the song came unbidden into her mind, with the rushing heart of a desert wind on Morningside, the passion of first love:

> Let me flower first for you
> Let me quench my thirst in you
> Share the best and worst with you. . . .

Her hands twisted, unconsciously; six rings of gold

slid against one another, circling her fingers, four on the left hand, two on the right.

> Husband, have me for a wife.
> You are the rain. . . .

She sagged against the wooden doorframe, shutting her eyes; pressed her face against the coolness, supported by its noncommittal strength. He was gone; they were all gone: her crew. her family . . . her husbands and her wives. Her strength, the strength that came from sharing, was gone with them, bled away into the bottomless void. How would she go on? Loss was too heavy a burden, life was too heavy a burden, to bear alone—

Something brushed her ankles; she opened her eyes, focusing. The cat wove between her feet, meowing forlornly. "Rusty—" She leaned down to pick the cat up, seeing the day of their departure from Morningside: the squirming, mewing kitten held out to her in the grubby hands of her daughter, Kiki, as all their children solemnly presented their chosen gifts to each and every parent. There had been a dozen grandparents looking on—and siblings, cousins, nieces and nephews, their proud, hopeful faces washed with ruddy light, the Darkside Perimeter's eternal twilight.

All of them were waiting—all of them were a part of her. The children were waiting; she was not alone. But they were all beyond her reach now, across too much space and time; and it was her duty, her responsibility, to get this ship back to them—

She heard a sound in the hall, straightened away from the doorframe with Rusty still nested in her arms. She saw Clewell, wearing only his shorts, standing in the doorway of his own room, watching her.

"Betha—are you all right?"

"Yes . . . yes, I'm just tired, Pappy." *Tired of remembering, and remembering. How can one sudden sorrow turn all my joy to pain?* Watching him back she saw the same desolation, the same wound of loss that tormented her. She felt her fear rise again, *Oh, Clewell; don't let me lose you, too.* "May–I share your room again, tonight?"

He nodded. "Please. I couldn't get to sleep anyway, alone."

She followed him into his room, and in the darkness unbuttoned her plain cotton shirt, slipped out of her shoes and jeans. She settled into the double sleeping bag beside him, into his arms, and put her own arms around him gratefully in a gesture of long familiarity. He had not been her first husband, but he had been her friend through more years than she could remember now. He had been twenty-seven the year she was born, one of many uncles; but from childhood on he had been her favorite among all the relatives of her extended family. He had been an astronomer before he had become navigator on the *Ranger;* he had traveled from Borealis on the chill perimeter of day, out across the Boreal Sea and over the crumpled ice sheet of the darkside glacier, to his observatory under eternal night. Sometimes he had taken her along for a brief holiday of stargazing, free from the duties and clan responsibilities that even a child on Morningside was expected to fulfill.

When she was fifteen she had gone away for her technical training; and then to her first job as an engineer, at a production plant on the desert edge of the subsolar Hotspot. She had fallen in love with Eric, married him; and in time they had returned to the Borealis moiety. She had reentered Clewell's life as a grown woman, and she and Eric had been invited to join his family.

Morningside society grew out of the multiple-marriage family, and bonds of kinship were its strength and security. Marriage among the members of a clan—a parent family, its children, their own children—was socially taboo; but outside the central clan unit, cousins, aunts and uncles, nieces and nephews married freely, their sheer numbers providing the cultural and biological controls. A marriage could be made between a single couple or a dozen people, and each family made its own rules to live by. Special friendships between individuals in a large family were common, and either the group as a whole adapted, or a subgroup split off. Weddings were a cause for general celebration, but divorce was a common, and private, matter for a family group. Three of the members of Clewell's family that Betha had known as a child had divorced the rest, and his first wife had died, before she and Eric had joined the group, and Claire, and Sean, after them.

Betha remembered the brief, fond ceremony of marriage, the immense, freeform family celebrations that had followed. All of Morningside loved a celebration, because too much of the time they had too little to celebrate. And now there would be even less, whether the *Ranger* ever returned or not. . . .

Betha became aware of Clewell's hand moving slowly, tenderly along her side. But the warm instinctive response of half a lifetime died in her. She buried her face against the pillow, smothering the words, "Oh, Clewell, I can't . . . I can't. Not yet. I'm so sorry. . . ."

His arms comforted her again, "No, Betha . . . it's all right. This is all I really need. Just to hold you."

She felt Rusty stir and settle between their feet at the end of the bed. She moved deeper into Clewell's arms, closing him in her own, and fled from memory into sleep.

LANSING 04 (LANSING SPACE) + 190 KILOSECONDS

The night stretched like silence beyond their searching eyes; they took comfort in its vast, star-flecked indifference. They were scavengers, picking the bones of worlds; the night gave them shelter because it made no judgments, and they were grateful for its amorality.

Shadow Jack watched the night, or its image on the screen . . . sometimes in the dim, close womb of the ship his mind blurred, and reality began to merge with image. He stretched his legs and scratched, brushed back the dirty hair that drifted forward into his eyes and was as black as the night before him on the screen. One eye was green and one was blue; both were bloodshot, and his head throbbed with his heartbeat. The carbon-dioxide level in the cabin was well over three percent; he had long ago stopped noticing the smells. He pulled himself back down into his seat, looking at one errant hole pricked in the darkness, the one star that was not a star—that was something infinitely more insignificant, and infinitely more precious.

"I think we're close enough to begin scan."

He heard Bird Alyn's voice, barely audible as always, even in the quiet space between them. He swallowed twice, wetting his throat for words. "Right. Go ahead an' run it through."

She reached forward with her right hand, her crippled left hand resting on air as she typed the order into the reconnaissance-unit computer that would begin one more analysis. Shadow Jack watched the long fingers with the broken, dirty nails move over the shining board. He looked away, for the ten thousandth time, at the cramped squalor of the cabin: still finding no miracle to transform the welded scrap-iron husk into a ship to match the technological beauty of the reconnaissance unit. Almost in apology, he smoothed fingerprints from the coolness of the panel with his frayed sleeve. The recon unit was a prize of salvage, a more precious thing than his own life, because it gave his entire world a chance for survival. Before the Civil War it had been a prospecting unit, programmed for laser and radar analysis of asteroidal metals, organics, volatiles. Now it scanned for the old instead of the new, searching the debris of death for artifacts to stretch the lives of the living. He looked back at the display with Bird Alyn, waiting, watched figures print out on the flat glossy screen—

"Nothin'," Bird Alyn said. "No metallic reflections, no radioactivity, no effluent across the surface . . . nothin', nothin', nothin'. Nobody ever lived there—"

"It's always nothin'!" He struck at the thick, darkened glass of the port, at a universe beyond his control.

"Maybe next time. Besides, maybe somebody else's found what they need. We're not the only ship . . ." She faded.

"I know that!" His voice battered his ears, he put up his hands. "I'm sorry. My head hurts."

"So does mine."

He glanced at her. It wasn't a reproach; her red-rimmed eyes were gentle, before they dropped away, fading against her face and the matted cotton of her hair, brown into brown into brown. Freckles splattered her nose, darker brown. "Do you think there's any water?"

"I'll see." He unstrapped and drifted up out of his seat, one bare foot pushing off from the panel. He reached the wall behind them, read the gauge on the still. "Yeah, there's some in it now." He heard Bird Alyn's sigh as he forced the nozzle through the seal on the drinking cup, waited while it filled. "Point four liters." He sighed, too.

They drank, taking turns at the straw, savoring the water's warm flatness; Bird Alyn reached over to turn down the display on the screen. She hesitated, leaned forward. "This's strange . . . look, the display's changed. There must be something else out there; we're getting a backscatter analysis of somethin' further on. Metal . . . low radioactivity . . ." Her voice rose until he could hear her without trying.

Bubbles of water burst against his fingers and slimed his hand as he squeezed the cup too hard. "A derelict?"

She tapped the controls briefly, and displayed a picture from the Matkusov mirror on the hull. A sunbright needle threaded stars on the blackness. "A ship," she whispered.

"Oh, reality, look at that. . . ."

"I never saw a ship like that. . . ."

"There's never been one."

"Not since the War. It's got to be—"

"It's got to be—salvage." Shadow Jack leaned forward, touched the ship with a wet fingertip. "I claim you, ship! With a ship like that . . . we could do anything with a ship like that."

"It's driftin', no propulsion. That doesn't mean it's dead. . . . To find that, here, so close to Lansing—"

"It is dead, it must be more'n two gigasecs old. What's our relative velocity? Can we intercept?"

Her long fingers asked the questions, the board answered. "Yes!" She looked up. "If we push, in four or five kilosecs."

"Okay." He nodded. "We push."

They waited, caught inside webs of private dream, as the needle of light grew into an impossible golden insect: triple antennae bristling ahead, spokes on an invisible wheel, its body stretching behind, filament-fine, and broadening into a bulbous, pearlike tail. *A miracle. . . .* The word shone in his mind, and knowing there were no miracles, he believed, defiantly. A ship that could get them water to fill the marshes, to bring back life to the parched grasses and dying trees . . . to the dying people of Lansing.

His mind's eye looked back into the past, down across Lansing's fields from the limits of the sky, where he had worked suspended cloudlike fifty meters up, spinning the sticky patches to mend the plastic membrane of the world-shroud. Somewhere below him through the fragile canopy of trees, Bird Alyn had worked in the gardens. . . . Like a vision of Old Earth, he remembered her crossing the yellowed fields at dusk to meet him, her footsteps lifting her like a bird. When they brought back that ship everything would be made right . . . everything.

He looked over at Bird Alyn, at her hand—three crooked, nerveless fingers and a thumb; felt her catch him looking. *Not everything.* He frowned with helpless self-disgust; she turned her face away as though the frown were meant for her. He looked out at the night, cracking his knuckles as he remembered why it would never be all right. He remembered the broken sound of his father's reassurance, a third of a lifetime before—as he left his only son sitting in the grass, abandoned to the fatal light, and went back into the sheltering depths of rock alone. . . .

RANGER (LANSING SPACE) + 195 KILOSECONDS

Betha heard the intruders banging faintly against the *Ranger*'s hull as they moved toward the main lock. "At least they didn't actually decide to cut their way in through the dayroom."

"Their manners don't impress me. You're just going to let them come aboard?" Clewell rebounded lightly from the wall as he pushed a covered cup into a cubby beneath the panel.

She nodded. "Pappy, we've been tracking that tin can of theirs for nearly two hours; it's hardly a warship. They must be in trouble—their drive is leaking radiation. Besides, we need information, and we haven't gotten much trying to monitor Lansing's radio traffic. Letting them come aboard is the safest, fastest way I can think of for getting some facts." She rubbed her eyes, until brightness drove back the vision of all her loves and one love, and the vision of a pursuing ship consumed by invisible fire. *Besides, there's been enough death.*

"And what happens if they happen to be crazy, like the others?"

"You said yourself they can't all be like that." Her hand closed over the bowl of her pipe. "But even if they are, they won't take the ship." She let the pipe drift as she rechecked the override program, a mosaic of lighted buttons on the control board. "Just keep your feet near the floor."

Someone had entered the lock. She felt more than heard them through the wall, felt her body tense as the lights changed above the lock entrance. The door hissed open. Two tall figures, amorphous in suits with shielded helmets, drifted into the room. And stopped short, catching at the handrail set into the wall. A muffled, accusing voice said, "What are you doin' here?"

Betha's mouth quivered; helpless with disbelief, she began to laugh. "W-what are *we* doing here?"

Clewell grunted. "We could ask you the same question; and it wouldn't be nearly as funny. You're lucky you're here at all."

"We thought the ship was dead; we didn't even know you had power till your lock cycled." The taller suit shrugged. "You've got a hole in you, and—you mean, you run this thing, you already claimed it?"

"We didn't 'claim' it, we own it." Betha caught her shoe under a restraining bar and twisted to face them. "I'm Captain Torgussen. This is my navigator. We let you come aboard because I thought you were in trouble. Your craft's power unit is leaking radiation; you're barely mobile. Is that why you intercepted us?"

The silvered faceplates showed her nothing, only her own tiny, distorted face. The voice was tinnily indignant. "What do you mean, leaking? There's nothin' wrong with our drive. We been out a megasec this trip, already."

Nothing wrong? Betha glanced at Clewell, saw his eyes widen. A megasecond—a million seconds—nearly two weeks. Whoever faced her, whatever insanity moved them, their lives were going to be short and sick spent in a ship like that.

The blind face went on, "We intercepted because we thought this ship was salvage, and we wanted it. I guess it's not." A gloved hand rose from his side, threatening, holding something that glinted. "But we have to have it. So we're taking it anyhow. Get away from those controls." The hand twitched.

"You'll regret it. The two of you can't possibly handle this ship." Betha carefully let go of the bar, her feet centimeters above the rug, her eyes on the panel. When she touched one button this room would be under an abrupt one-gravity acceleration: one stranger would fall onto his head, the other one onto his back. . . . *And break their necks?* She hesitated. "If you think—"

A blob of mottled fur squeezed out of a plastic port in the wall; Rusty *mrr*ed pleasantly, circling the knees of the two strangers. Betha heard one of them gasp. He pulled back, bouncing off his companion. "Look out!" Rusty darted sideways eagerly, enjoying the game. "What is it?" Their voices rose. "Shadow Jack, get it off me!"

Betha jerked the computer remote from her belt and threw it. It struck the stranger's arm and his weapon flew out into the room. Clewell moved past her to pick it from the air; the hijackers pressed back against the wall, waiting.

"Rusty. Come here, Rusty," Betha put out her hand, and brindle ears twitched. Slowly Rusty crossed the room to sidle along her waist, purring in satisfaction. Betha scratched under the ivory chin, stroked the brindle back, shaking her head. "Rusty, you make fools of us all."

"Well, I'll be damned!" Clewell began to pry at the weapon; strange shapes bristled along its length. "This is a can opener! Corkscrew, fork . . . I don't know what this one is. . . ." He pulled himself down. "I've heard of ailurophobes, but I've never seen the likes of those."

Betha caught hold of a chair back, unsmiling. "You two. Get out of the suits." They stripped obediently, rising like moths from the cocoons of their spacesuits: a man and a woman . . . a boy and a girl, incredibly tall and thin, neither of them more than seventeen; barefoot, in drab, stained coveralls. She blinked as the smell of them reached her. "You've just committed an act of piracy. Now tell me why I shouldn't send you out the airlock for it, without your suits." She wondered if the threat sounded as credible or as terrible as she wanted it to.

The boy glared back at her, across a muffled fit of coughing. The girl moved away from the wall. "It was a matter of life and death." Her voice was strained in a dry throat.

"We offered you help. That's not good enough."

"Not *our* lives." She shook her head. "We need the ship for . . . for . . ." She broke off, her eyes darted away, searching the room.

"Bird Alyn, they know why we need the ship." Betha saw a terrible, impersonal hatred settle on the boy's face as he turned back. "You know what we are. We're just junkers, we haven't done anything to you. Let us go."

Betha laughed again in disbelief. "You 'just' tried to commandeer my ship. I 'just' asked you why I shouldn't space you for it. But you expect me to let you go? Is everyone in Heaven system crazy?" Her voice almost slipped out of control.

"It doesn't matter." He let go of the handhold, shrinking in on himself. "We'll die anyway. Everybody's dying. You've still got it good, you Demarchists. It's nothing to you to let us go, or let us die."

Betha found her pipe drifting, fumbled in a pocket of her jacket for matches. "We're not 'Demarchists,' whatever they are. We've come from another system to establish contact with the Heaven Belt; and since we've been here we've been attacked twice, with no provocation, near the rings of Discus and by you.

Now, maybe you believe you had some sort of 'right' to do it, and maybe you can even make me believe it. Or maybe I'll take you to Lansing to be tried for piracy." She saw surprise on their faces. "But first you're going to answer some questions. . . . To begin with: who are you, and where do you come from?"

"I'm Shadow Jack," the boy said, "and this's Bird 'Alyn. We come from Lansing." He waited.

"But that's where we're going—" Clewell began.

"*Why?*" The girl said, blinking.

"Because it's the government center for Heaven Belt." Betha looked back at her sharply. "Your capital must have come on hard times."

"You really are from Outside, aren't you?" Shadow Jack folded his legs like a buddha, somehow managing not to flip over backward. "There hasn't been any Heaven Belt for two and a half gigasecs."

"What?"

He stared, silent; Clewell gestured threateningly at the cat.

"There was a war, the Civil War. Everything got blown up, all the industry. Nobody can keep anything going any more, except the Demarchy and the Ringers. They're the only ones far enough out to have snow on some of their rocks. Lansing is capital of zero, nothin'; most everybody in the Main Belt's dead by now."

"I don't understand," Betha said, not wanting to understand. *Oh, God, don't let our very reason for coming here have been pointless. . . .* "We heard that Heaven Belt had the perfect environment, that it had a higher technology than any Earth colony, than even Old Earth."

"But they couldn't keep it goin'." Shadow Jack shook his head.

Betha saw suddenly the fatal flaw the original colonizers, already Belters, must never have considered.

Without a world to hold an atmosphere, air and water—all the fundamentals of life—had to be processed or manufactured or they didn't exist. And without a technology capable of the processing and manufacturing, in a system without an Earthlike world to retreat to, any Dark Age would mean their extinction.

As if he had followed her thoughts, Shadow Jack said, "We'll all be dead, in the end, even the Demarchy." He looked away, forcing out the words, "But our rock is out of water now. Everybody there'll die if we have to go around Heaven again without it. And we don't have a ship left that'll take us to the Ringers—to Discus—for hydrogen to make more. We've got to find enough salvage parts to put one together. That's why we were out here. It's a gigasec before we'll be close enough to Discus to make the trip again."

"You trade with Discus for hydrogen?" Clewell broke her silence.

"Trade?" Shadow Jack looked blank. "What would we trade? We steal it."

"What happens if the—Discans catch you in their space?" Clewell reached under the panel for his covered drinking cup, pulled up on the straw.

Shadow Jack shrugged. "They try to kill us. Maybe that's why they attacked you: they thought you came from the Demarchy. Or maybe they wanted your ship; anybody'd want this ship. Can you run it all with only two people—?" His mismatched eyes wandered speculatively.

"Not two untrained people," Betha said, "in case you still have any ideas. It's not even easy for us. There were five more people in our crew; the Discans killed them all." *And all for nothing.*

He grimaced. "Oh." Betha saw the girl flinch.

"One more question." She took a deep breath. "Tell

me what this 'Demarchy' is, that everyone seems to confuse with us."

Shadow Jack glanced away, suddenly oblivious, as Clewell finished his drink. Bird Alyn licked her lips, rubbed her mouth with a misshapen hand.

Out of water. . . . A memory of her own children, too far away, too long ago, dimmed their hungry faces. She looked down at her own hands, at thin golden rings, four on the left hand, two on the right. "Well?"

Shadow Jack cleared his throat, his eyes daring her to offer water. "The Demarchy—it's in the trojan asteroids sixty degrees ahead of Discus. It's got the best technology left now. They made the nuclear battery that runs our electric rocket; they're the only ones who can make 'em any more."

"If they're so well off, why do they have to rob the Discans?"

"They don't have to. Usually they trade, metals for the processed snow, for water and gases and hydrocarbons. Sometimes things happen, though—incidents. They both want to come out on top. I guess they think someday they'll build up the Belt again. They're wrong, though. Even if they'd quit fightin' each other, it's too late. Anybody can see that."

"Not exactly a cockeyed optimist, are you, boy?" Clewell said.

Shadow Jack frowned, scratching. "I'm not blind."

"Well, Clewell." Betha felt Rusty snuffling against her neck, settled the cat on her shoulder. Claws hooked cautiously into the weave of her denim jacket. "What do you think? Do you think it's the truth? Did we—come all this way for nothing?"

He rubbed his face with his hands. She saw his own wedding bands reflecting light, three on the left hand, three on the right. "I guess it's possible. It's so insane, it's the only way to explain what we've been through."

She nodded, glanced at the haggard faces of the waiting strangers: *Not exactly angels.* Victims, of a tragedy almost beyond comprehension; a tragedy that had reached into her own life, and his, to destroy the dreams of another people as it had destroyed its own. This Heaven, like all dreams of heaven, had been a fragile thing; perhaps none of them had ever been meant to be more than a dream. . . . She lit her pipe, calmed by its familiarity, before she searched the two tense, expectant faces. "I'll make you a proposition, Shadow Jack, Bird Alyn. You said Lansing needs hydrogen for water; we need it for fuel. We're going after it now. Come with us and tell us things we need to know about this system, and if we succeed we'll share what we get with you."

"How do we know you'll keep your word?"

Betha raised her eyebrows. "How do we know you've told us the truth?"

He didn't answer, and Bird Alyn frowned at him.

"If you're honest with us, we'll be honest with you." Betha waited.

He looked at Bird Alyn; she nodded. "I guess anythin's better than our chances alone. . . . But what about the *Lansing 04?* We can't junk it—"

"We can take your ship with us. It's possible we can repair your shielding."

His mouth opened; he shut it, embarrassed. "We—can we radio home, Lansing, and tell 'em what happened?"

"Yes."

"Then, its a deal. Well stick with you, and tell you what we know." They relaxed visibly, together, hanging like rag dolls in the air.

Clewell folded his arms. "Just keep one thing in mind—that the captain meant it when she told you it takes training to run the *Ranger*. We'll be accelerating at one gravity. Even if you took over the ship and contacted your people, they'd never catch up with you. All you'd get out of it would be a one-way journey to forever."

Shadow Jack started to answer, kept silent.

"I'll see to your ship, then. Clewell, will you take them below? Maybe, ah . . ." She looked back; tactfulness eluded her. "They could use a shower."

"A shower of what?" Bird Alyn murmured.

Betha paused, inhaling smoke. "Well . . . water."

"Unfortunately we're out of champagne." Clewell pushed off for the doorway.

Shadow Jack laughed uneasily. "Enough water to wash in?"

She nodded. "Use all you want; please. We have plenty. And soap. And clean clothes, Clewell–"

"With pleasure." He led them eagerly out of the room into the echoing stairwell; Rusty floundered after them. For a moment Betha drifted, listening, her eyes taking in the grass-greenness of the rug, the dust-blue sky color of the walls, that had been designed to keep seven people from going mad during more than three years tau of close confinement. She realized the vast and pernicious emptiness that had filled the room, the entire ship, in the past few days; like the greater desolation beyond its hull. Realized it, now that suddenly it was no longer true. She heard the sprayers go on, and faint yelps of excited laughter.

Clewell reappeared in the doorway, carrying Rusty. "I hope they don't drown themselves . . . though anything would be an improvement."

She looked down at the pipe in her hand, remembering how he had carved it for her during their final days in Borealis. Surprising herself, she began to smile.

RANGER (IN TRANSIT, LANSING TO DEMARCHY) + 290 KILOSECONDS

Bird Alyn moved slowly through the green light of the *Ranger*'s hydroponics lab, her frail body twitching with the effort of standing upright in one gravity. She hummed softly, oblivious to discomfort, pulled into the past by the cool constant moistness and the smell of apples, the hum of insect life. Shadow-dapples slid over the tiles, merging and breaking with the drift of canopied leaves, showering sparks of veridian fire over the viscous liquid inside clear, covered vats.

The setting was strangely alien, like everything in the bountiful alien wonderland of this starship. But a fern or a tree were always the same, no matter how gravity or its lack contorted them. They were living things that required her—that rewarded her care and attention with a leaf or a blossom or fruit to give her people life. The only living things that willingly absorbed all the love she could give them, that never turned away from her because she was an ugly, ungainly cripple. . . .

Bird Alyn drew the dipstick out of another vat, studied the readings, shook it down. She sighed and slid down the vat's side to sit on the floor, massaging her swollen feet. They prickled, with the sluggishness of poor circulation. She leaned back, looking up through the shifting green; imagined she saw the milky translucency of the Lansing shroud and

Shadow Jack working as a spinner, instead of the banks of fluorescent lights.

She had counted the kiloseconds, the very seconds of every Lansing day, until Shadow Jack came down to join her for the day's one meal. Silent, moody, filled with futile anger—he was still the one person in her world who responded to her, who pushed out of his own shadowed world each day long enough to show her kindness. Sometimes she wondered whether he was kind out of pity; never caring whether he was. She was simply grateful, because she loved him, and knew that love had no pride.

From childhood she had understood that she would work in the surface gardens; through all of her life she had seen why—that she was different, deformed. Her parents had trained her to use a computer, because they had accepted that she would have to work at a job where the radiation level was high; they had equipped her to work on a ship, to do the best she could for the survival of her world. But beyond that they had withdrawn from her, as people withdraw from a mistake that has ruined their lives, as they withdraw from the victim of a terminal disease.

And she had never questioned her own inferiority, because Materialist philosophy taught her that every individual must accept the responsibility for his own shortcomings. She had gone to work on Lansing's surface almost gladly; glad to escape from the world of normal people, glad to lose herself in the beauty of the gardens, solitary even among her fellow defectives.

And then she had discovered Shadow Jack sitting dazed and frightened in the grass at the entrance to the tunnels. . . . Shadow Jack, who had grown up used to a normal life of security and acceptance. Who had been told, suddenly, that he was not normal, and cast out into an alien world, ashamed, abandoned. She had comforted him, out of compassion and her own need; his need had bound him to her, and made them friends.

But as they grew older she began to want more than just his friendship; even though she knew that it was wrong, and impossible. On the Lansing surface the mores of the tunnels were distorted by neurosis, or by need, until each person became literally responsible for his own actions, and endured whatever consequences followed. She had seen things that would have appalled her parents, and learned to see that they did no one any harm; to see that that was the only real criterion for what was right or wrong. And there were things that had made her afraid, once she understood them, and grateful that Shadow Jack slept beside her every night in the sweet cool grass or between the sheltering pillars of the abandoned state buildings.

But Shadow Jack would never touch her, never let her ease the anger and the helpless resentment that never let him go. And helpless in her own futility, she kept her silence, knowing that it was wrong for a defective to want a husband; impossible, that Shadow Jack could ever love an ugly, clumsy cripple. . . .

Bird Alyn saw someone draw aside the insect netting and enter the lab, brushing aside grasping shrubs and vines. She struggled to her feet, trying to make the figure into Shadow Jack . . . heard a woman's voice call softly, "Claire?"

Bird Alyn stood on tiptoe, fading against the flowers in her green shirt and blue jeans. "What?" She teetered and almost dropped the dipstick. She clutched it against her side with her crippled hand. "Oh, Betha."

Betha stared at her in return, shook her head, bemused and disconcerted.

Bird Alyn smiled, glancing down. "I—I thought it

was Shadow Jack. He said he was goin' to come watch me work. . . ." Her smile collapsed.

"Pappy's got him cornered; he's showing him around up in the shop." Betha touched a fern, pulled off a yellowed frond, pulling the dead past loose from the present. She looked back, concern showing on her tired, pale face. "Are you sure you want to do this, while we're still at one gee?"

Bird Alyn nodded. "It's all right. I sit down a lot, and just—watch, and smell, and listen. It's so long since I worked in the gardens. Do you mind?"

"No . . . no. You don't know how much I appreciate it. There's enough work on this ship for seven people. And—Clewell's not as young as he used to be." The captain's eyes left her, searching the green shadows. "You have the perfect touch, Bird Alyn . . . I almost took you for a dryad when I came in."

"What . . . what's that?"

"An enchanted forest spirit." Betha smiled.

"Me?" Bird Alyn twisted the dipstick, laughed her embarrassment. "Oh, not me. . . . These plants take care of themselves, really, it's easy . . . not like Lansing . . . they look so different here, so thick and squat. . . ."

"These?" Betha looked up.

"On Lansing things keep growin' up, they don't know when to quit; it's tricky, the root systems have to go down to bedrock and catch hold . . . and with the mutations . . ." Bird Alyn faded, suddenly aware of her own voice.

Betha sat down in a tiled bench, reached out for the strangely shaped thing half-hidden under a fall of vine. "Claire's guitar. Claire used to run hydroponics, and she used to play for the plants. It's a musical instrument," seeing Bird Alyn's puzzled expression. "We all used to come down here in the evenings, and sing. She used to claim the plants enjoyed the music, and the emotional communion. Of course, Lara would claim it was just the carbon dioxide they wanted . . . and Sean said it was the hot air." Her mouth curved wistfully. "And Eric—Eric would say that it was probably a little of everything. . . ." Her hand rose to her face; Bird Alyn counted four plain golden rings, surprised, before it dropped again.

"How . . . um, how does it work?" She had known a girl once who had a whistle made from a reed. "The—guitar, I mean." She leaned back against a heavy wooden shelf, pushed up onto its edge with an effort.

"I can't really give you a proper idea, Claire was an artist; I only know a few chords. But it's something like this. . . ." The captain settled the guitar across her lap, positioned her fingers on the strings. She stroked them tentatively.

Bird Alyn shivered. "Oh . . ."

Betha smiled; her fingers changed position on the strings and the shimmering water of sound altered. She began to sing—almost unconsciously, Bird Alyn thought—in a warm, clear voice merging with the flow of music:

> "Understanding comes from learning
> No one ever changed a world.
> Live your life, don't waste it yearning,
> You can't change it, little girl—"

Bird Alyn felt her throat tighten, looked down at her twisted hand, blinking hard.

She heard the captain take a long breath, caught in her own memories. "I'm sorry." The clear voice strained slightly. "I should have found something a little more cheerful."

"Please . . . will you—will you do some more?" Bird Alyn looked up.

Betha's face eased. "All right . . . they aren't much, just some old folk tunes. But it's a strange thing, the effect that everyone singing together has—the bond that grows between you, the feeling of unity. It gives you the strength to carry on, when things are hard. And it's hard to hate anyone when you're singing with them; hard to be angry. . . .

"Together we continue,
Our song will never end.
Sister, brother,
Father, mother,
Share their lives with one another:
Woman, man and friend. . . ."

Bird Alyn leaned forward, like a flower leaning into the light. "Morningside must be a beautiful place!"

Betha made a sound that was not quite a laugh. "No, it's . . . Yes. Yes . . . in a way. In its own way." Her fingers brushed the strings again.

"I wish I could do that. . . . Do you . . . know any love songs?" The captain looked up sharply; Bird Alyn realized that somehow she had said the wrong thing.

"I'll be glad to show you what guitar chords I know, Bird Alyn, if you want to learn to play. Maybe the plants miss it."

Bird Alyn folded her arms. "I—I don't think I have enough fingers. . . ."

The captain's face froze with a second's embarrassed awkwardness. "Oh. Well, I think I can reverse the strings for you; I've seen a guitar played left-handed before. If you'd like me to?" She smiled again.

"Oh, yes!" Bird Alyn slipped down off of the shelf, left the dipstick hanging absently in the air. It slid through her nerveless fingers and clattered to the floor. Instinctively a long bare foot stretched to pick it up; she lost her balance, and fell. "Lousy luck!"

Sprawled on the floor, she fumbled after the rod, shook it and checked the readings, while a familiar hot flush crept up her face.

The captain came to her, caught her arms and lifted her effortlessly to her feet. "Are you all right?" Betha's hand brushed her arm reassuringly, as a mother might have touched her. "It takes a while, doesn't it, to break the habits of a lifetime."

Bird Alyn looked down, confused by her solicitude. "Does anybody ever get used to this? If you're not born used to it, I mean. . . ."

Betha stepped back. "In time. Morningside's pull is less than one gee, but we've been at one gee on the ship for three years, and we don't even notice the difference any more. I've read some Old World studies on one-gee adaptations from low gravity. It's possible, but it takes about a year—thirty or forty megaseconds—to get back to the minimum endurance you had at zero gee. And there are long-term stress effects on the body. But they decided that you'd last, with good medical care, if you wanted to go through with it."

"I think I'd rather go home," Bird Alyn said.

"Me too." Betha nodded.

But you can't. Bird Alyn glanced down at her, blushing again. "I mean . . . I always say the wrong thing!"

"No. It's all any of us want, Bird Alyn. And we're going to do it." Betha studied the pattern of gleaming rings on her hands; they tightened suddenly.

Bird Alyn listened to water dripping somewhere, thought of tears. She heard someone else enter the lab; recognized Shadow Jack this time.

Betha smiled, a pleased, private smile, following her glance. She turned back to the bench, picked up the guitar. "I'll change the strings for you, when I get the chance. But now I'd better get back to work. We're almost into Demarchy space; you won't have to put up with gravity much longer." She started away toward the door, spoke to Shadow Jack as she passed him. Bird Alyn watched his own gaze fix on her, follow her, with admiration that was almost adoration. Bird Alyn felt envy stir, turned it inward habitually. Her mouth tightened with pain as though she had turned a knife.

But Rusty struggled in Shadow Jack's arms, meowing with sudden impatience as they caught sight of her. Shadow Jack let the cat drop, still half afraid of its strangeness. Rusty trotted ahead to butt against Bird Alyn's bare ankles; Bird Alyn leaned over and picked the cat up, and a pink tongue sandpapered her chin joyfully. Rusty settled, purring, onto her shoulder. She thought of the embroidered hanging in the room that was hers now: a cross-stitched portrait of Rusty, and the words, A HOME WITHOUT A CAT MAY BE A PERFECT HOME, PERHAPS—BUT HOW CAN IT PROVE ITS TITLE? Bird Alyn let herself imagine an entire world filled with living creatures, and music; not a fruitless dream, but reality. The kind of world Lansing must have been, in the time she had never known; the kind of world it could never be again.

"I thought Rusty was looking for you," Shadow Jack murmured, self-conscious. "I'll bet if there were ten animals on this ship, every one would want to be with you."

She met his eyes hesitantly, forgetting everything in the miracle of his smile.

FLAGSHIP UNITY (DISCAN SPACE)
+ 300 KILOSECONDS

Raul Nakamore, Hand of Harmony, settled back into the padded acceleration couch, weightless, held down by straps. He wedged the light wire headset into a slot on the panel, through with the radio, through arguing with his half-brother Djem. So he was wasting the Grand Harmony's resources . . . risking his life . . . risking the crews of three ships to pursue a phantom. So he was leaving Snows-of-Salvation unprotected from a Demarchy attack to chase a ship that could run rings around the ships of the Grand Harmony, even this high delta-vee strike force. A ship from Outside . . . a crippled starship, that had left behind a tiny spreading cloud of debris and human remains. A ship that had eluded their grasp once—but that might not be able to do it again. It was worth the gamble. *But poor Djem; he never could see beyond the end of his own nose.* Raul half-smiled.

Somewhere five thousand kilometers below him, silhouetted against the silvered detritus of the Discan rings, the lump of frozen gases that was Snows-of-Salvation held the Grand Harmony's chief distillery. It had been constructed with Demarchy aid, and it was crucial to the Harmony's survival, and the Demarchy's. His brother was in charge of Snows-of-Salvation, would do anything to maintain its safety. But if the Demarchy decided to attack here in the Rings, even this "secret weapon" couldn't stop them from doing fatal damage. And in spite of what too many in the Navy believed, the Demarchy would never try it, anyway. Djem would never be able to see that, but Raul would stake his career on it—*had* staked his career on it. The Demarchy would never attack them . . . unless it had that starship. But if the Grand Harmony took it first—

"Sir." Sandoval, the balding ship's captain, interrupted his pattern of thought diffidently. "Everything's secure for ignition. At your command—"

Raul nodded, unbuttoning his heavy jacket in the unaccustomed warmth of the control room. *Been underground too long. . . .* He sighed. "Proceed."

Sandoval settled back into his own seat, spoke orders into his headset that would coordinate with the crews of two other ships. There was no video communication; video was used only to impress the enemy. Raul studied the complexity of the control board, banks of indicators spreading up the walls in the cramped space around them. Most of it was prewar artifact computing equipment, installed to give these ships superior maneuverability in combat. They were one segment of the Grand Harmony's high delta-vee defense force, specially designed, specially equipped with a fuel-to-mass ratio of one thousand to one. Although Raul Nakamore ranked in the highest echelons of the Harmony navy, he had always maintained that their existence was pointless waste of desperately needed resources; and for that reason he had never been on board one of these ships before. But now the starship had changed his mind; as it could change the very future.

He sank heavily into the padded seat as the ship's liquid-fuel boosters ignited and thrust grew to a steady two gravities, more than slightly painful on his Belter's frame. He checked the chronometer on the panel. Thrust would continue for thirteen hundred seconds, boosting them to sixteen kilometers per second . . . and in that time, expend seven thousand tons of fuel: the outer stages of the three ships themselves, and of seven drones. And still it would take them over two megaseconds to reach Lansing—and their quarry might not even be there. Raul settled down to wait, trying not to imagine the waste, but rather to remember what had made him so certain it was worth it. . . .

He had been sitting in his office, studying endless shipping schedules, when the confidential report had reached him: a ramscoop starship, origin unknown, had crossed the path of a naval patrol . . . and had destroyed one of their ships before escaping. He had studied the report for a long time, with the warmth of the methane stove at his back and the chill silence of Heaven's future ahead of him. And then he had noticed that a meeting was announced, his presence was required.

He left his office and made his way along the endless dank, slightly smoky corridors from the Merchant Marine wing. The government complex made up the greater part of the tunnel-and-vacuole system that honeycombed the subsurface of the asteroid Harmony, that had been the asteroid Perth in the time before the Civil War, before the founding of the Grand Harmony. The chill began to eat its way through his heavy brown uniform jacket; he pushed one hand into his pocket, using the other to push himself along the wall. He was a short man, barely 1.9 meters, and stocky, for a Belter. There was a quality of inevitability about him, and there had been a time when he had endured the cold better than most. But he was a career navy man, and he had spent most of his adult life on ships in space, where adequate heat was the least of their problems. But for the past sixty megaseconds since his promotion he had been an administrator, and learned that the only special privilege granted to an administrator was the privilege of managing a double workload.

He passed through large open chambers filled with government workers, into more hallways identical to the ones he had just left, into more chambers—as always experiencing the feeling that he was actually traveling in circles. Unconsciously he chose a route that took him through the computing center, guided by past habit while he considered the future. The past and the present surprised him as he became aware of his surroundings: of the crowded rows of young faces intent on calculation, or gaping up at his passage.

He looked toward the far corner of the chamber, almost expecting to find his own face still bent over a slate of scribbled figures. He had worked in this room, twelve-hundred-odd megaseconds ago, starting his career while still a boy as a computer fourth class. A computer in the oldest sense, because the sophisticated machinery that had borne the Discans' burden of endless computations had been lost during the Civil War. After the war, the Grand Harmony had learned the hard way that it would never survive without precise data about the constantly changing interrelationships of the major planetoids. And so they had fallen back on human computation, using the inefficient and plentiful to replace the efficient but nonexistent, as they had had to do so many times.

A bright child could learn to do the simpler calculations, and so bright children were used, freeing stronger backs for heavier labor. Raul remembered sitting squeezed onto a bench with another boy and a girl, huddled together for warmth. His nose had dripped and his lips were chapped, and he had stared enviously at the back of his half-brother Djem, who was one hundred and fifty megasecs older and a computer second class. The higher your rank, the closer you sat to the stove in the center of the room. . . . By the time Djem made first class, Raul had joined him, and been rewarded with warmth and one of the few hand calculators that still worked.

Their common grandfather had proved Riemann's Conjecture, and become the best-known mathematician—and perhaps the best-known human being—to come from the Heaven Belt; but then the war had come, and made him only one more refugee. He had been on vacation in the Discan rings when the war began, and his loyalties had been suspect. But his mathematical skill had been undeniable—and now, two generations later, the residue of his genius had put his grandsons on the path to success in a new regime.

"Only through obedience do we earn the right to command. . . ." Raul left the computer room, and his youth, behind; the universally colorless moral admonitions from the inescapable wall speakers crept back into his consciousness along with the cold. He wondered how long it would be before the news of the alien starship worked its way into the communal broadcasts, between the Thoughts from the Heart and the lectures on Demarchy decadence—and what form it would take when it did. He did not object to the constant intrusion into his life. He was used to it. It was as much a part of the life he knew as the cold. He realized that it served a purpose, distracting the people from the cold and the endless dreary labor of their daily lives, reinforcing their sense of unity and dedication to the group.

But if he felt no resentment toward the broadcasts, neither did he take them seriously any more. He had realized long ago that they were just as much propaganda as the Demarchy's own lurid displays of unharmonious advertising. . . . The Demarchy, that still lived in warmth and comfort—thanks to the distilleries of the Grand Harmony—but which kept the people of the Grand Harmony from sharing that comfort. It refused to sell them the atomic fission batteries that were still the Demarchy's major source of power, for heat, for light, for shipping, for the few factories that still operated. No existing factories operated at more than one percent efficiency in the Grand Harmony—except for the distilleries—and virtually their only source of heat and light came from the inefficient burning of methane (because the Rings had a surplus of volatiles, but that was all they had).

Raul pushed the thought out of his mind, as he pushed aside the more painful truth that his people, all the people in Heaven Belt, were doomed. Regret was useless. Hatred was counterproductive. Raul faced the truth, and faced it down. He saw the road ahead clearly, saw it grow steeper and more difficult until at last it became impossible. But he moved ahead, one step at a time, strengthened by the knowledge that he had done all that was humanly possible.

There had been a time when he had absorbed every word of the broadcasts, and believed every word. He had hated the Demarchy then, with the blind passion of youth; and because he was young and competent and expendable, he had been sent on a mission of sabotage into Demarchy space. And he had failed in his mission. But to his intense humiliation, the perversity of the Demarchy's media-ruled mobocracy had transformed him into a popular hero, taking his impassioned last denunciation of their own aggression to heart . . . and the Demarchy had sent him home, a shamefaced messenger of goodwill, to open negotiations for the construction of a distillery that would benefit both the Demarchy and the Grand Harmony.

But relations between the Harmony and the Demarchists had never improved past that one act of cooperation, the real purpose of which lay in their shared needs: independent Demarchy corporations still violated Discan space, and only their overall economic weakness kept them from outright seizure of the Harmony's vital resources. The Grand Harmony still denounced the Demarchy, and blamed it for its own marginal existence.

But because of his experience in the Demarchy, the conviction that good and evil were as easily marked as black and white, that every question had a simple answer, had been lost to him forever. And as he came to see that the Demarchy was not totally evil, he had realized that it was not totally to blame for the Harmony's precarious survival, either. He had come to see the greater, totally amoral and totally inevitable fate that drew the Grand Harmony, and the Demarchy as well, down the road of no return.

And when he had seen that there was no turning back, no turning aside, he had transferred from Defense to the Merchant Marine; to serve where he believed he could function most effectively, and make the Harmony's passage down that road as easy as possible.

Raul reached the hub of the government complex at last, felt the eddies of cold draft catch him as he moved out into the suddenness of open space. Overhead the ceiling was dark and amorphous, but he knew that its vault was a surface of clear plastic, not solid stone. Once it had opened on the stars, and the magnificence of Discus—when the Rings of Discus had been the water-well for the entire Heaven Belt. But now the clear dome was blocked beneath an insulating pack of snow; the dome had become too great a source of heat loss.

He made his way across the multiple trajectories of other drifting government workers, most of them navy men like himself. He returned their raised-hand salutes automatically, his mind reaching ahead of him into the restricted meeting room where his fellow Hands sat in a private conference with the Heart.

Raul settled quietly into his seat, waiting for the meeting to be called to order. He sat at the end of the long table farthest from the position of the Heart, as the newest officer to achieve the rank of Hand. He nodded to Lobachevsky on his right, looked past, identifying the faces of officers and advisers down the table. He noted without surprise that they had split into opposing factions, as usual—the defense faction on one side, the trade faction on the other. He had settled with the trade faction, as usual. Seeing the bare, shining tabletop as a kind of no man's land between them, he smiled faintly.

A single word silenced the muttered speculation; Raul turned his attention to the head of the table, rose with the rest, acknowledging the arrival of the Heart—the triumvirate that controlled power's ebb and flow in the Grand Harmony. Chatichai, Khurama, and Gulamhusein: like a many-faceted Hindu deity, indistinguishable from one another, or from their staff, in the drab sameness of their bulky clothing . . . but unmistakably set apart by an indefinable self-satisfaction—and the unharmonious ambition that had taken them to the top, and made them struggle to stay there. Raul knew the kinds of stress that worked on them, and was grateful that he had already risen above the level of his own ambitions.

The three men at the head of the long table settled slowly onto the seat, a sign for the officers to do the same.

"I assume you all read the communications that brought you here"—Chatichai spoke, taking the initiative as usual—"and so I assume that you all know that fifty kiloseconds ago our navy encountered a ship like nothin' that exists anywhere in this system. . . ." He paused, looking down; Raul recognized a tape recorder on the table before him. "This's a report from Captain Smith, who was in charge of the patrol fleet that encountered the craft." He pressed a button.

Raul drifted against the table, listening, and watching expressions change along the table's length. They had taken the intruder for a Demarchy fusion ship violating Discan space, at first. Then, as they began to close and a woman's voice answered their challenge, they realized that what they had come upon was something totally unexpected. The ship had broken away from them, accelerating at an impossible sustained ten meters per second squared; it had destroyed one of their own closing craft almost casually, with nothing more than the deadly effluence of its exhaust. But they had fired on the escaping ship, and they had recorded a small, expanding cloud of debris. . . .

An undercurrent of irritation and excitement spread along the table. "Why the hell didn't Smith give that woman port coordinates, when she asked for 'em?" Lobachevsky muttered beside him. "Damn sight more reasonable than tryin' to take the ship by force. Losin' a ship—serves him right." He glared across no-man's-land at the opposition. Raul kept his own face expressionless.

Chatichai raised his eyes, and his voice. "The question before us now, gentlemen, is not whether Captain Smith acted in the best interests of the Grand Harmony—but what further action should be taken concernin' that ship. I don't think anybody here will disagree that the ship had to come from outside the system. . . ." He paused; no one did. "And I don't think we have to detail for anybody here what a ship like that could mean to our economy . . . or to the

Demarchy's, if they get hold of it instead." Another pause. "But is it feasible, or even possible, for us to get our hands on that ship? And in any case, what action should be taken to ensure that it doesn't fall into the Demarchy's hands instead?"

Raul studied the dull sheen of the table's scarred plastic surface, seeing beyond it as he listened with half-attention to the debate progressing along the table's length: the ship was damaged . . . the ship could still outrun anything that Heaven Belt could send after it. The ship might seek out the Demarchy because of the attack . . . there was no reason to believe its crew would trust anyone in the Belt, now. The ship was the answer to the Harmony's survival . . . the ship was a phantom, and pursuing it would only waste more resources they couldn't afford to lose. . . .

Raul glanced up, pushing his own thoughts into order. He rarely spoke out unless he had been able to consider all sides of a question; he had learned long ago that selective silence was a more effective tool than a loud voice. Since his promotion to Hand, he had used it to good effect to earn himself a reputation for getting what he wanted, for building up the efficiency of the Merchant Marine and the influence of the trade faction. Finding a lull, he broke into the discussion: "As you all know, I've been opposed to the development and support of our high delta-vee force from the beginnin'. . . ." He searched the faces along the table, seeing resentment glance along the far side, feeling the gratification that spread from Lobachevsky along his own side. He had believed, along with the minority of others, that the Demarchy posed no realistic threat to the safety of the Grand Harmony, that the resources used to maintain a defense fleet would serve the Harmony's interest better if they were employed to bolster trade within the Rings, and even with the Demarchy itself. Because he understood that the status quo was deterioration, and that nothing could overthrow that order. . . . "But this's a situation I never forsesaw. In this situation, I have to admit I'm glad we have a high delta-vee force available . . . and I am in favor of usin' it to pursue that ship—" Voices indignant with betrayal cut him off; he saw the hostility re-form into surprise across the table. "I know it's a gamble. I know it's probably a futile one, the odds against us capturin' that ship are damned high. But they're not astronomical: the ship's damaged, we don't know how severely. It may be that they'll lie low at Lansing, if Lansing's still alive; it's worth the loss, worth the gamble, to find out. We've got this damned high delta-vee force whether we want it or not—let's put it to some rational use! If we know this much about the starship, you can count on the Demarchy knowin' just as much—and bein' just as interested. I don't believe they're any threat without that ship; but if we don't get the ship, and they do, anything we do is goin' to be academic from then on.

"I propose that the closest available high delta-vee force be readied as soon as possible to pursue the starship toward Lansing. And I request that I be given command. . . ."

The acrimony of the final debate faded from his mind as acceleration's false gravity abruptly ceased, leaving his body free in a sudden release from tension. He had won, in the end, because there was no one in the room who could question his sincerity, or his determination to achieve whatever goal he set himself. And so these ships would continue in a drifting fall toward Lansing. And if the life-support systems held out, they would find—something; or nothing. The cards had been laid down; the Grand Harmony had gambled on the last chance it would ever have.

RANGER (DEMARCHY SPACE)
+ 553 KILOSECONDS

"No, that won't work either. They could see this isn't a prewar ship." Bird Alyn shook her head; her hair, caught into two stubby ponytails, stood out from her head like seafoam.

"Then there's nothing more I can suggest, offhand." Betha glanced from face to face, questioning. Clewell sat firmly belted into a seat; Bird Alyn and Shadow Jack sprawled in the air, totally secure in the absence of gravity. The five-day journey along sixty degrees of Discus's orbit had transformed them, superficially: Their skin and hair were shining clean, their long, gangly bodies forced into dungarees and soft pullover shirts. But the start of one-gee acceleration had left them crushed on the floor like reedflies, and they still winced with the stiffness of wrenched muscles, and the memory. And there were other memories, that shone darkly in their hungry eyes and quick, nervous words; memories out of a past that Betha was afraid to imagine and glad she would never know.

"I still say you should leave the Demarchy alone." Shadow Jack stuck out a thin bronze foot, stroked Rusty gingerly as she drifted past. "We should've gone for the Rings. It's a lot safer to steal it from them. If you ask me—"

"I wasn't asking—that." Betha smiled faintly. "I want to trade, not steal. . . . I already know how 'safe' it is in the rings of Discus, Shadow Jack."

"But the Demarchy's worse. They've got a higher technology."

"How much higher? You don't really know. And they aren't looking for us, either. With your ship to ferry us in, we can slip in and out of a distillery before they even think about it. But what do we trade for hydrogen?" She repeated the inventory again in her mind, struggling with the knowledge that only Eric would know what was right, what to offer, what to say. Only Eric had been trained to know. . . . *Oh, Eric—*

Shadow Jack frowned, pulling at his toes. Bird Alyn caught Rusty, set her spinning slowly head over paws in the air. Rusty caught her own tail and began to wash it. Bird Alyn laughed, inaudible.

"The cat," Shadow Jack said. "We could give them the cat!"

"What?" Clewell straightened indignantly.

"Sure. Nobody's got a cat any more. But nobody in the Demarchy could know we didn't; Lansing had a lot of animals, once. And it's just what the Demarchists go for: somethin' really rare. The owner of a distillery, he'd probably give you half his stock to own Rusty."

"That's ridiculous," Clewell said.

"No . . . maybe it's not, Pappy." Betha spread her hands, and Rusty pushed off toward her. "I think he's got a point. Rusty, would you like to live like a queen?" She gathered Rusty into her arms, gathered in the precious memories of her children's faces, as they handed her the gifts of love. She felt her throat tighten against more words, wondering what payment would be demanded next of them; knowing that whatever the emotional price was, they must pay it, if it would buy this ship's passage home to Morningside. She saw sharp sorrow on Bird Alyn's face; saw Bird Alyn struggle to hide it, as she hid her own. "Besides

. . . we haven't been able to think of anything else that wouldn't give us away. Any equipment we tried to trade would be obvious as coming from outside the system. We'll be taking enough of a risk as it is."

"I know." Clewell looked down. "You're the captain."

"Yes, I am." Betha pulled herself down to the control panel, tired of arguing, tired of postponing the inevitable. There was no choice, there was only one thing that mattered—saving this ship—and she must never forget it. . . . She watched the latest surveillance readouts, not seeing them. The *Ranger* was well within Demarchy space now. They had detected dozens of asteroids and heavy radio traffic. They had identified Mecca, the largest distillery, eight million kilometers away, with a closing velocity of ten kilometers per second—only hours of flight time for the *Ranger*. But it would take the *Lansing 04* two weeks, decelerating every meter of the way, to close the distance-and-velocity gap between them and Mecca. Her stomach tightened at the prospect; the extra shielding they had put on board the Lansing ship cut the radiation levels to one-sixth of what they had been, but the readings were still too high. And yet if the *Ranger* came any closer to an inhabited area, the risk of detection would be too great.

> The road to Morning
> Is cut from mourning,
> And paved with broken dreams. . . .

"I'm going to Mecca, Pappy," she said at last. "I'm going to get us our ticket home."

Clewell sat firmly in his seat as Bird Alyn floated

free above his head. They watched together while the *Lansing 04*, a battered tin can with a reactor tied to its tail, fell away into the bottomless night. He looked back from the darkness to Bird Alyn's face, her own dark eyes still fixed on the screen. "I'm glad you're here. There's too much—emptiness on this ship, alone."

She blinked self-consciously, her arms moving like bird wings as she turned toward him in the air. Her eyes rarely met his, or anyone's; as if she was afraid of seeing her own image reflected there. "I wish—I wish she hadn't taken Rusty."

He had to strain to hear her, wondered again if he was getting a little deaf. "So do I. She did what she thought was best. . . . And you wish she hadn't taken Shadow Jack."

She still looked down; her head twitched slightly.

"She did what she thought was best." He thought of Eric, who had been trained to know what was best; remembered Betha's anguished doubt, in the private darkness of their room. "She means everything to me, too."

Bird Alyn looked up at him at last. "Are—are you Betha's father?"

He laughed. "No, child; I'm her husband. One of her husbands."

"Her—husband?" He almost thought he could see her blush. "*One* of her husbands? How many does she have?"

"There are seven of us, three women and four men." He smiled. "I take it that's not so common here."

"No." Almost a protest. "Are . . . the rest of them back on your—planet?"

"They were the crew of the *Ranger*."

She jerked suddenly. "Then—they're all dead, now."

"Yes, All. . . ." He stopped, forcing his mind away from the empty room on the next level below, where a gaping wound opened on the stars. Deliberately he looked back at Bird Alyn, saw her embarrassment. "It's possible to be in love with more than one person, you know."

"I always thought that meant somebody had to be unhappy."

He shook his head, smiling, wondering what strange beliefs must be a part of the Lansing culture. And he wondered how those beliefs could survive, when a people were struggling for their own survival.

On Morningside the first colonists had struggled to survive, expatriates and exiles fleeing an Earth where the political world had turned upside down. They had arrived in a Promised Land that they discovered, too late, was not the haven they were promised—discovering at last the lyrical irony in the name Morningside. Tidally locked with its red dwarf star, Morningside turned one face forever toward the bloody sun, held one side forever frozen into night. Between the subsolar desert and the darkside ice lay a bleak ring of marginally habitable land, the Wedding Band . . . until death did them part. The fear of death, the need to enlarge a small and suddenly vulnerable population, had broken down the rigid customs of their European and North American past. They were no longer the people they had once been, and now, looking back across two hundred years of multiple marriage and the freedom-in-security of extended family kinship, few Morningsiders saw reason in their own past, or any reason to change back again.

Bird Alyn folded her arms, hiding her misshapen hand. And Clewell realized that perhaps the people of Lansing had had no choice in their customs either. If the radiation levels were as high as those on the *Lansing 04*, even one percent as high, then the threat of genetic damage could force them into breeding customs that seemed strange or even suicidal anywhere else. The whole of Heaven Belt was a trap and a betrayal in a way that Morningside had never been: because Heaven had promised a life of ease and beauty in return for a high technology, but it damned human weakness without pity.

Clewell was silent with the realization that whatever Morningside lacked in comfort, it made up for in a grudging constancy, and that even beauty became meaningless without that. . . .

"How did you and Shadow Jack end up out here?"

She shrugged, a tiny waver of her weightless body. "I can work the computer; my parents programmed the recon unit. And Shadow Jack wanted to be a pilot and do something to help Lansing; he won a lottery."

"Your parents let you go, instead of going themselves?" He saw Betha suddenly, in his mind: a gangly, earnest teenage girl, helping him take the measure of the immeasurable universe . . . saw his own children, waiting for him across that universal sea. He covered a sudden anger against whoever had sent their half-grown daughter out in a contaminated ship before they would go themselves.

Bird Alyn looked down at her crippled hand. "Well, you can only go if you work outside. . . ."

"Outside?"

"Lansing's a tent world . . . we have surface gardens, an' a plastic tent to keep in an atmosphere." She ran her hand through her hair, her mouth twitching. "You work outside if you can't have children." For a moment her eyes touched him, envious, almost accusing; she turned back to the viewscreen, looking out over isolation, withdrawing into herself. "I think I'll take a shower."

He laughed carefully. "If you take too many showers, girl, you'll wrinkle up for good."

"Maybe it would help." Not smiling, she pushed off from the panel.

He looked out at the barren night, where all their hopes lay, and where all the dreams of their separate worlds lay ruined. Pain caught in his chest, and made him afraid. *Help me, God, I'm an old man. Don't let me be too old. . . .* He pressed his hands against the pain, heard the sprayer go on and Bird Alyn's voice rise like warbling birdsong, beginning a Morningside lullaby:

"There's never joy but leads to sorrow,
Never sorrow without joy.
Yesterday becomes tomorrow;
I can't stop it, little boy. . . ."

LANSING 04 (DEMARCHY SPACE)
+ 1.51 MEGASECONDS

"There it is," Shadow Jack said, with almost a sigh. "Mecca rock."

Betha watched it come into view at the port: a fifty-kilometer potato-shaped lump of stone, scarred by nature's hand and man's. Mecca's long axis pointed to the sun; the side nearest them lay in darkness, haloed by an eternal corona of sunglare. As they closed she began to see landing lights; and, between them, immense shining protrusions lit from below, throwing their shadows out to be lost in the shadow of the void. She identified them finally as storage tanks—enormous balloons of precious gases. *At last* . . . She stirred in the narrow, dimly lit space before the instruments, felt her numbed emotions stir and come alive. She filled her congested lungs with the dead, stale air, heard a fan go on somewhere behind her, clanking and ineffective; wondered whether she could ever revive a sense of smell mercifully long dead. It was small comfort to know that the claustrophobic misery of their journey would have been worse without the overhauling they had done on board the *Ranger*. Two strangers from Lansing could teach even Morningsiders something about toughness. . . . The *Ranger* came back into her mind, and with it the galling knowledge that they could have crossed Demarchy space to Mecca in one day instead of fifteen, in perfect comfort—if things had been different. "But we're here. Thank God. And thanks to you, Shadow Jack. That was a good job." Her hand stroked his arm unthinkingly, in a gesture meant for someone else. He started out of his habitual glumness, looking embarrassed and then something more; reached to scan the radio frequencies. Static and voices broke across the cabin's clicking silence.

"Did—did you love one of them best?"

She sighed. "Yes . . . yes, I suppose I did. It's something you can't help feeling; I loved them all so much, but one . . ." *Who isn't here, when I need him.* She shook her head, her eyes blurred, and sharpened again as a piece of the real world moved across them. "Out there, Shadow Jack." She leaned closer to the port, rubbed the fog of moisture from the glass. "A tanker coming in."

He peered past her. They saw the ship, still lit by the sun: a ponderous metallic tick, its plastic belly bloated with precious gases and clutched inside three legs of steel, booms for the ship's nuclear-electric rockets. "Look at the size of that! It must be comin' in from the Rings. They wouldn't use that on local hauls." He raised his head, following its downward arc. "Down there, that must be the docking field."

She could see the field clearly now, an unnatural gleaming smoothness in the artificial light, cluttered with cranes and ringed by more mechanical parasites, gorged and empty. Smaller craft moved above them, fireflies, showing red; sluggish tows in a profusion of makeshift incongruity. *Another world* . . . She listened, watching, matching fragments of one-sided radio conversations with the movements of the slow-motion dance below them: boredom and sharp attention, an outburst of anger, unintelligible humor about an unseen technicality. "Shouldn't they be receiving our signal?"

He nodded. "They are. I guess they'll call us down when they feel like it."

Rusty stirred in the air above the control board, batted listlessly at the twined cord of his headset. "Poor Rusty," Betha murmured, reaching out. "Your trip in this sauna is almost over. . . ." The rawness of her throat hurt her suddenly.

Shadow Jack twisted guiltily, stroked Rusty's rumpled fur. "Bird Alyn really let me have it for makin' you take Rusty away. She didn't want to lose her. She loves plants, makin' things grow—things that are alive. . . ." His mouth twitched, almost a smile, almost sorrow. "I guess Rusty was about the most wonderful thing of all, to Bird Alyn."

"You miss her."

"Yeah, I . . . I mean, well, she's the only one who can really use the computer."

"Oh."

He glanced back at her, knowing what she hadn't said. "We just work together."

She nodded. "I thought maybe you—"

"No, we don't. We're not married."

She felt her mouth curve up in scandalized amusement. "I admire your self-restraint."

His blue and green eyes widened; she saw darkness settle across them again. "There's no point in wanting what we can't have. It's only keeping alive that matters—everybody keeping alive. If we can't get water for Lansing, then it's the end, and it's stupid to pretend it's not. There's no point in . . . in . . ." He looked down at the control panel. "Those daydreamers! Why don't they answer us? What do they need, a miracle?"

A voice broke from the speaker, "Unregistered ship—what the hell are you doing up there, running so dark?"

Shadow Jack turned back to her, speechless; she smiled. "Now try wishing for hydrogen."

Shadow Jack took them in, cursing in the glare, to a moorage on Mecca's day side. " 'Not registered for main field.' Those nosy bastards! How come we couldn't land in the dark, like the rest of those damn charmed tankers?" He stretched, leaning back, and cracked his knuckles.

"I suppose they don't want some tourist crashing into the distillery." Betha relaxed at last, at the reassuring sound of magnetic cables attaching to the hull outside.

He pushed himself away from his seat. "That doesn't help us. If something goes wrong, we'll have a hell of a time gettin' out of here this way." He moved toward the locker that held their spacesuits.

She sighed and nodded, reaching out to catch Rusty. "We'll just hope nothing goes wrong," thinking that whoever had named him for shadows had named him well.

Betha clung momentarily to the edge of the open airlock, looking down, and away, to where the world ended too suddenly: the foreshortened horizon, like the edge of a gleaming, pitted knife blade against the blackness. And beyond it the stars, scarcely visible, impossibly distant across the lightless void. She saw five torn bodies, falling away into that void where no hand could stop their fall, where no voice could ever break the silence of an eternity alone. . . . She swayed, giddy. Shadow Jack touched her back.

"Go on, push off." His voice crackled, distorted by his feeble speaker.

Behind his voice in her receiver she heard Rusty's fruitless scratching inside the pressurized carrying case; she saw figures coming toward them, moving along a mooring cable fastened amidships. She pushed herself out of the hatchway with too much force, drifted through a graceless arc to the ground. She began to rebound, caught at the mooring line and steadied herself. *A mistake* . . . And she couldn't afford to make another one. She was dealing with Belters, and she'd damn well better act like the Belters did. She felt tension burn away the fog of her exhaustion, as she watched Shadow Jack land easily on the bright, pockmarked field of rubble behind her. Above him she saw the sun Heaven, a spiny diamond in the crown of night, frigid and faraway—bizarre against the memory of her sun's bloody face in a dust-faded Morningside sky. As she turned away from the shadowed hull of the *Lansing 04* she could see other ships moored; the stark light etched the crude patchwork of misshapen forms on her mind, overlaying her memory of the *Ranger*'s ascetic perfection.

"You staying here long?"

She couldn't see the port man's face through the shielding mask of his helmet; she hoped her own faceplate hid her as well. "No longer than we have to."

"Good; your exterior radiation level's medium-high. Not good for the plants."

She looked down at the stained rubble, wondered if he was making a joke. She laughed, tentatively.

"You're the Lansing people?" Eight or ten more figures spilled out from behind him, with bulky instruments she realized were cameras.

"What are you here for?"

"Is it true that—"

"I thought everybody in the Main Belt was dead?"

She shifted Rusty's case, getting a better grip on the cable; their voices dinned inside her helmet. "We want to buy some hydrogen from your distillery." She looked back at the port man. "I hope we don't have to walk to the other side?"

He laughed this time. "Nope. Not if you're paying customers."

Betha noticed that he was armed.

". . . heard you Main Belters mostly scrounge and steal," the voices ran on. "Have you really got somethin' there to trade for snow?"

"How is it that a woman's in your position; are you sterile?"

"What's in the box?"

They surrounded her like wolves; she drew back, appalled. "I don't–"

"That's for us to know, junkers," Shadow Jack said suddenly. "We're not here for handouts. We don't have to take crap from any of you." He caught the guard's rigid sleeve. "Now, how do we get to the distillery?"

Betha's jaw tightened, but the guard raised his hands. "All right, you media boys, get off their backs. Take a picture of the ship; they didn't come from Lansing to pose for you. And be sure to mention Mecca Moorage Rentals. . . . No offense, buddy. Just follow the cable back to the shack; they're holdin' the car for you. Welcome to Mecca."

"Say, is it true that–"

Shadow Jack drifted over the cable and pushed past them to the far side. Betha followed, her motion painfully nonchalant. "Thanks–buddy," she said.

The guard nodded, or bowed, and so did Shadow Jack.

"Christ, who *were* those people?" She glanced over her shoulder as they boarded the single canister car of the ground transport; behind them someone sealed the door. She heard Shadow Jack mutter, "Unreal." There were two others in the cabin, she saw, wishing it was empty, glad there were only two and hoping they didn't have cameras. Ahead through the plastic dome, the filament-fine monorail track stretched away over the barren brightness. Beyond the platform on her right she saw what looked to be a circular hatchway set into the surface of the rock; above it was a sign: HYDROPONICS CO-OP. She realized that the guard hadn't been making a joke; the chunk of naked stone that was Mecca was a self-sufficient world, riddled with tubes and vacuoles that supported life and all its processes. Too much radiation was bad for the plants. . . .

Her thoughts jarred and re-formed as gentle inertia pressed her against the seatback. Rusty snuffled and scratched in the carrier, making a sound like static inside her helmet; suddenly, painfully, she remembered their destination, and their purpose. And that only Eric could help her now—but Eric was gone. "I wonder if this was built before the war?" She glanced at Shadow Jack's mirrored faceplate, needing an answer.

"Yes, it was." The voice in her helmet belonged to a stranger.

She started; so did Shadow Jack. They turned to look at the two others in the car; one, long legs stretching casually, reached up to clear his faceplate. "Eric—!" Her hand rose to her own helmet, hung motionless, almost weightless.

Curling dark hair, a lean, pensive face; the sudden smile that was almost a child's. The brown eyes looked surprised . . . amber eyes . . . not Eric, not . . . *Eric is dead.* She pulled down her trembling hand, leaving her faceplate dark. "I—I'm sorry. I thought . . . I thought you were someone I knew."

He smiled again, politely. "I don't think so."

"You're the ones who came to trade, from Lansing." The second voice rasped like grit. "They said the car was waiting for you."

Betha winced, unseen. She looked across at the shorter, somehow bulkier figure; wondered if it was possible to find a fat Belter. Her own 1.75 meters felt oddly petite. The woman cleared her helmet glass, showed a middle-aged face, brown skin and graying hair, eyes of shining jet.

"Yes, we are." Betha kept her faceplate dark to hide her paleness, felt Shadow Jack fidget beside her.

"You're the first ones I've ever seen from the Main Belt. What's it like back in there? It's good to learn that you aren't all—"

Rusty emitted a piercing yowl of desolation, and Betha gasped as it rattled against her ears.

"My Lord, what was that?" The woman's gloves rose to her own shielded ears.

"Ghosts," Shadow Jack said, "of dead Belters."

The woman's face went blank with confusion. Betha glanced at the man, saw him smile and frown together; he met her unseen eyes. "Never heard a noise like that. Maybe we passed over a power cable." She realized that not only the cat, but the carrying case transmitter must be an unheard-of novelty in Heaven now.

The woman looked shaken. "I'm sorry. That wasn't gracious of me, anyway. Just that you're such a novelty. I'm Rinee Bohanian, of Bohanian Agroponics." She gestured at the sunside behind them. "Family business, you know."

"Wadie Abdhiamal." The man nodded. "I work for the Demarchy."

"Don't we all?" the woman said.

"The government."

She peered at him with a suspicion edging on dislike. "Well." She looked back at Betha. "And what's your name? You know, I'd like to get a look at a genuine spacewoman—"

"Betha Torgussen. I'm sorry, my helmet's broken." She crossed her fingers; no one showed surprise. "And this is—"

"Shadow Jack," Shadow Jack said. "I'm a pirate."

"Pilot," Betha murmured, irritated, but the others laughed.

"That's a Materialist name." The man was looking at Shadow Jack. "I haven't met one of those in a long time."

"Everybody's one, on Lansing. But it's just wishing. Nothin' left to contemplate." He was almost relaxing, the hard edge softening out of his voice.

The man glanced at Betha, questioning.

"Not everyone." She turned away toward the front of the car, looking for a reason to stop talking. She heard the woman asking the man what he did for the government, didn't listen to his reply. They were nearing the terminator; it ran smoothly to meet them, like a cloud shadow crossing the broken desert lands of Morningside. Beyond the terminator, parallel to the edge of shadow, lay a line of leviathans: stubby poles of steel crowned by rings of copper, strung with serial blinking lights, red and green.

"That's the linear accelerator," the woman said. "It's used to ship cargo that doesn't have to move too fast, or go too far. . . . What exactly does a Materialist think?"

They crossed the terminator, blinking into night as though a switch had been thrown, and passed between the looming towers of the accelerator. The dark-haired man sat listening to Shadow Jack; unwillingly Betha felt her eyes drawn back to his face.

". . . and you're given a word, the name of somethin' material that's supposed to set each of you apart and shape your being somehow. Half the people don't even know what their words mean, now. . . ."

She watched the stranger in silence, helpless, flushed with sudden radiance, chilled until she trembled. . . . Remembering Morningside, the first days of her love for Eric: remembering an engineer and a social scientist ill-met in a factory yard on the Hotspot perimeter, and blazing metal in the unending heat of endless noon. . . . Remembering their last days on Morningside: a film of ice broken in a well in unending dusk, where the crackling edge of the darkside ice sheet, stained with rose and amber by the fires of sunset, shattered its mirror image in the Boreal Sea. Borealis Field, where her family, as the newly chosen crew of the *Ranger*, worked together preparing for an emergency shipment, preparing themselves for the journey across 1.3 light-years to icebound Uhuru.

They had been selected from all the volunteers willing to leave homes and jobs because another world in their trade ring needed help; but they had never imagined the journey that in the end would be assigned to them. Word had come from the High Council that a radio message had been received from Uhuru, and aid was no longer needed. They had been given a new, unexpected destination, the Heaven system, and a goal that was more than simple survival for another world or their own. She remembered the celebration, their pride at the honor, their families' families' pride. . . . Remembered Eric leading her quietly from the crowded, fire-bright hall, for one brief time alone before a journey that would last for years. His gentle hands, and the caressing heat of the deserted sauna; their laughing plunge into banked snow . . . the heat of passion, the wasting cold of death . . . fire and ice, fire and ice. . . . She cried silently, *Eric, don't betray me now. . . . Give me strength.*

The car slipped on through darkness.

The car drifted to a stop beneath the slender towers of their destination, among the ballooning storage sacs that glowed with ghostly foxfire—dim yellows, greens, and blues, excited by the ground lights into a strange phosphorescence. Betha shook off the past, looking out into the glowing forest of alien shapes. She heard the woman: ". . . how your Lansing fields are like our tank farmin'. Of course, there's no shortage of water for us; we have the snow stored below in the old mining cavities. We've got enough to last forever, I expect." A pride that was unconsciously greed filled her smile. The government man glanced at her; Betha saw him show quick anger and wondered why. Shadow Jack pushed abruptly up out of his seat, stabilized himself instinctively. Tension tightened him like a wire again; she wondered what showed on his face.

They followed the man and woman through disembodied radio noise and the impersonal clutter of workers on the platform, came to another hatch set into the solidness of the surface rock. Below the airlock they entered tunnels that sloped steeply downward, without seeming to, into the heart of the stone. Betha felt her suit grow limp with the return of air pressure, making her movements easy. Sounds carried to her now, dimmed by her helmet, as she passed new clusters of citizens, some suited and some not, all mercifully oblivious; she wondered again at the behavior of the cameramen on the field.

They followed a rope along the wall of the main corridor, where the rough gloves of pressure suits had scraped a shallow trough along the pitted surface. Ahead and below she saw the tunnel's end, opening onto a space hung with fine netting. Curious, she drifted out onto the ledge at the chamber's lip.

"Oh . . ." Her breath was lost in a sigh. She stood as Shadow Jack already stood, transfixed by a faery beauty trapped in stone. Before them a vacuole opened up, a kilometer or more in diameter: an immense, unnatural geode filled with shining spines of crystal growth, blunt and spike-sharp, rainbow on rainbow of strident, flowing color. The hollow core of air was hung with gossamer, silken filaments spread by some incredible spider. . . .

The images began to re-form in her mind; she realized that this was the city, the heart of life in the Mecca asteroid—that the crystal spines were its towers, reaching up from the floor, out on every side . . . down, from the ceiling. *Why don't they fall—?* Her thoughts spun, falling; she felt someone's hands clutch her arms. Her mind settled, her feet settled softly on the ledge. Angrily she forced her eyes out again into the chamber's dizzy immensity. People drifted, as tiny as midges, along the gossamer threads; light ropes, strung across the wide, soft spaces. The towers grew thickest, probing the inner air, on ceiling and floor, in the direct line of gravity's faint inexorable drag. The buildings that hugged the hollow's curving sides were shorter, stubbier, enduring greater stress. The towers shivered delicately in the slight stirring currents of ventilation; they were not solid crystalline surfaces, but trembling tents of colored fabric stretched over slender metal frames.

"It was a 'model city' before the war." She saw that the government man was the one who had caught her arms; he released her noncommittally. "It used to be a gamin' center. Now we play more practical games; most of those towers belong to merchant groups." The man unlatched his helmet, lifting it off and looking at her expectantly. "The air's okay here."

She reached up only to switch on her outside speaker; her skin prickled, wanting the touch of his eyes. "Thank you"—she tried to sound unsure—"but I'll wait." Shadow Jack, speakerless, stood looking out into the city, sullenly content to play deaf and dumb. "Can you tell us which of those belongs to someone who can sell us hydrogen?"

"Hydrogen?" His wandering glance leaped back to her shielded face. "I thought you'd want air. Or water."

"We do. We need water—we have oxygen. So we need hydrogen, obviously." Rusty yowled; she closed her ears.

"Oh." His face relaxed into acceptance. "Obviously. . . . You know, it's not often that I meet a woman who's chosen to go into space. Is it common on Lansing?"

"Going into space isn't common on Lansing, any more." Betha remembered suddenly that the stranger's golden-brown eyes belonged to the enemy. "If you could just point out the distillery offices for me?"

"Down there"—he pointed—"that cluster of long greens on the floor; lot of offices for the distilleries in that bunch. Tiriki, Flynn, Siamang . . ."

"Distilleries? There's more than one?" *Should I have known*? She swore under her breath.

"Sure are." But he smiled, tolerantly. "This is the Demarchy, the people rule; we don't like monopolistic practices. It infringes on the people; they won't stand for it. . . . I know. Let me take you around."

"No, really—"

"It's the least I can do, when you've come this far." He put two fingers into his mouth and whistled shrilly, three times. She flinched; he turned back to her, surprising her with a quick, apologetic bow. "That's how you call a taxi here, now. Mecca's manners are going to hell. . . . Heaven is going to hell."

He laughed oddly, as if he hadn't expected to say it out loud. "I'm from Toledo, myself."

"What–ah–did you say you do for the government?" She looked away uneasily across the ledge. The woman from the train had disappeared. *Why is he staying with us like this?*

"I'm a negotiator. I try to keep things from getting any more uncivilized than they already are." Again the quick, pained laugh. "I settle disputes, work out trade agreements . . . look into unexpected visits."

She almost turned, froze as she saw the cameramen from moorage emerge from the tunnel. "Shadow Jack!" She caught his arm. "Stay with me, don't get separated."

The voices closed in on them, ". . . in that run-down ship?"

"Who are you making your deal with?"

"How much–"

"What do you have–"

Mediamen and staring locals crowded them, ringed them in, jostling and interrupting. She saw the government man elbowed aside as the air taxi drifted up to the ledge, grating to a stop. She pushed toward it, gesturing to Shadow Jack. It was canopied and propeller-driven, steered by hand by a bored-looking, well-dressed boy. "Where to?"

"To–to Tiriki's. And hurry." She ducked her head at the edge of the striped canopy, felt the footing bob beneath her in a sea of air, seeing crystals reflecting above and below. Shadow Jack followed. The taxi sank outward and down, away from the grasping mob on the precipice.

". . . Torgussen!" She heard the government man shouting after her.

She looked back; her hands rose to her helmet, fumbling, pulled it off. She saw his face change with incredulity . . . recognition . . . loss. . . . *Stop it!*

There was no resemblance, there could be no recognition . . . *Eric is dead!* She clung to a canopy pole, feeling the air currents stir her pale, snarled hair, soothe her burning face. *Oh, God, how often will this happen?* Shadow Jack hung over the edge, looking down, up, sideways, as they passed the artificial sun caged in glass suspended in the cavern's center. Slowly she sank onto a seat, forcing her own senses to absorb her surroundings, jamming the echoes of the past.

The cavern was filled with sound, merging and indistinct: laughter, shouting, the beehive hum of unseen mechanisms. She looked ahead, aware now of subtle differences of richness and elaboration among the massed towers; of balconies set at insane angles; of dark hollows in the bedrock walls, tunnels to exclusive homes. And gradually she became aware of the mingling of spices that perfumed the cool filtered air; she breathed deeply, tasting it, savoring it, easing her stuffy head. Unimpressed, the driver stared through her at the emerald pinnacle of their destination.

They pushed through the soft elastic mouth of the roof entrance, into a long empty corridor stretching twenty-five meters down to the building's base on rock. Betha began to sink toward it, almost imperceptibly, and with no sensation of falling; they began to pass doorways. Shadow Jack unlatched his helmet, pulled it off and shook his head. She heard him take a deep breath. "Where are we?" His hair was plastered like streamers over his wet face; he wiped it back with a gloved hand.

"Tiriki Distillates. The man from the train suggested it." She hesitated, not wanting to tell him what she suspected.

"Bastards." His mouth pulled back. "I'd like to see this place blow up. They wouldn't be so–" Anger choked him.

Betha watched him, feeling sorrow edged with annoyance. She reached out; her glove pressed the soft, resistant covering on his shoulder. "I know how you feel . . . I know. But so did the people in that train car. Take the chip off your shoulder, right now, or I'll knock it off myself: I can't afford it. I want something from these people, and so do you, and it's a hell of a lot more important than what either one of us feels. So put a sweet smile on your face while we make this deal, and keep it there if it gags you." Somewhere the memory broke loose: " 'Smile and smile . . . and be a villain.' " She smiled, breathing the cool scented air, and willed his eyes to meet hers. Slowly he raised his head; as he looked at her, for the first time, she saw him smile.

Someone pushed through a doorway almost at her side. He caught the flap, looking at her with frank disbelief.

She rubbed her unwashed face, embarrassed. "We'd like to negotiate for a load of hydrogen. Can you tell us who to see?"

A mask of propriety formed. "Of course. Sure. At the far end of the hall, the Purchasing Department. And thanks for doing business with Tiriki." He ducked his head formally and moved past them, pushing off from wall to wall, rising like a swimmer through the brightening sea-green light. They went on down, into the depths.

"Look at this rag." They heard the voice before they reached the doorway. "What do they know about it? They don't know a damn thing."

"No, Esrom."

Betha brushed aside the flaps and they went in, wearing smiles rigid with tension.

"I could do better myself. That's what we ought to do, do it ourselves. We ought to hire some mediamen and put out our own paper—"

"Yes, Esrom."

"—tell them our side. Look here, Sia, 'monopolistic' . . ."

The golden-skinned, ethereally beautiful woman behind the counter looked up at them; her arching eyebrows rose. The golden-skinned, strikingly handsome man with the printout turned. *Brother and sister*, Betha thought, *and . . . impeccable.* They wore soft greens, colors flowing into a background of sea-green light, the woman in a long embroidered gown, the man in an embroidered jacket, lace at his sleeves. She pictured what they saw in return, brushed at her stringy hair.

But the man said, "Sia, did you ever see anything like that? Look at that skin, and hair, together. . . ." His dark eyes moved down her suit, identified it, looked back at her face. "But she's been in space." Interest faded to regret.

The woman tapped his arm. "Esrom, please!" She charmed them with a smile. "And what can we do for you?" She smoothed her sinuously drifting, raven-black hair along her back, tucked strands under her lacy cap.

"We'd like to buy a load of hydrogen from you." Betha felt herself blushing crimson while they watched in fascination. She tried to hide her annoyance. "One thousand tons."

"I see." The man nodded slowly, or bowed, looking vaguely surprised. He reached for a clipboard on a chain. "Do you want it shipped?"

"No, we can move it ourselves."

"Where are you coming from?" The woman's voice was as fragile as her face, but with no hint of softness.

"Lansing." Shadow Jack smiled, tall and thin and genuine, with one blue eye and one green.

"The Main Belt!" Brother and sister looked at them again; silent, this time, with a morbid awe. A newscast appeared on the screen behind them, flashing pictures between lines of print. "That's quite a trip," the man said quietly. "How long'd it take you?"

"A long time." Betha gestured up at worn, dirty faces, not needing to force the grating weariness into her voice. "And it'll be even longer going home. We'd like to get this settled as soon as we can."

"Of course." He hesitated. "What–er, what did you want to offer in trade? We're limited in what we can take, you understand. . . ."

Charity begins at home. She saw Shadow Jack's rigid smile twitch, as she pulled off her gloves. *But who am I to blame them for that?* She balanced Rusty's carrying case against the metal counter top and unsealed the lid, hearing the hiss as the pressure equalized. Rusty's mottled head rose over the edge, her dilated pupils black with excitement, flashing green in the light. Her nose quivered and she wriggled free, rising up into the air like a piece of windborne down. Betha heard the small gasp of the woman, and let the case drift away. "Will you take a cat?"

"An animal," the woman whispered. "I never thought I'd ever see one. . . ." Shyly she put out a hand. Betha stroked Rusty, reassuring, pushed her toward them. Rusty butted softly up against the woman's palms, sniffing daintily, sidling in pleasure along the fine satin cloth of her sleeve.

"I think you've come to the right place." The man's slender hands quivered. "Dad would give you the whole distillery for that animal." He laughed. "But he'd make you pay shipping in to the Main Belt."

"Are there many animals left on Lansing?"

"No." Betha smiled, felt it pull. "A load of hydrogen will be fine."

"We have gardens," Shadow Jack said. "Lansing's the only tent rock. We were the capital of all Heaven Belt, once." He lifted his head.

"Sure," the man said. "That's right, it was. I've seen pictures. Beautiful . . ."

Rusty slipped away from the woman, began to jab a paw through the holes of a mesh container for papers. The papers danced and she began to purr, smugly content at the center of the world's attention. Betha's eyes were drawn away to the newscast on the wall; she froze as she saw her own face projected on the screen, realized it was not coverage of their arrival on Mecca. With all her will she glanced casually away, reaching out to scratch Rusty under the chin.

The man caught her motion, turned to look up at the screen. Her eyes leaped after him, saw her image vanish into lines of print. The man looked back at her, puzzled; shook his head, grimacing politely. "Don't mind the screen. We like to get the news from all over, to see what the competition's up to. It's all static anyhow—mediamen'll say anythin' they're paid for." He gestured at the printout settling gradually into a heap on the counter. Rusty pounced, overshooting, and swept it out into the air.

"Here, little thing, don't hurt yourself," the woman murmured, her hands tightening with indecision.

"She'll be all right," Betha said, irritable in her relief.

A small disapproval showed on the woman's face.

"Do you mind if we take a look at your ship?"

Betha looked back at the man. "No . . . but it's at the other end of the ast—of the rock."

He nodded. "Easy to do." There was a small control panel under the wall screen; he moved away toward it. "What's your designation?"

"*Lansing 04.*"

He changed settings, and the news report vanished. "*Lansing 04* . . ." Betha saw their ship appear, an image in blinding contrasts on the sunbleached field. "I guess it's possible for you to move a thousand tons with a ship that size. How much does it mass?"

"Twenty tons without reaction mass or cargo."

"We like to be sure, you know." He looked up. "It's goin' to take you a lot of megasecs, though, to get back to Lansing."

She watched his face for unease, saw only his easy solicitude. "We'll manage; we have to."

"Sure." His eyes moved from her to Shadow Jack, touching them, she saw, with a kind of admiration. "We'll start processing your shipment."

Rusty crashed against the counter edge in a snarl of printouts and sneezed loudly.

"Hey, now." The man turned away, reaching for Rusty almost desperately. "Dad would kill us if somethin' happened to—" His voice faded, he let her go, catching up a sheet. Betha saw her own face on the page between his hands, not disappearing this time. ". . . alien starship . . ." She heard Shadow Jack's soft curse of defeat. She drifted, clutching the counter edge until her fingers reddened.

The Tirikis turned back to her. "It's you," the man said, staring. "You're from the starship."

"And you've come to us."

An unconscious smile spread over their faces, the look of guileless greed Betha had seen on the woman in the shuttle. "I don't understand," she said stubbornly. "You've seen our ship; we've come from the Main Belt. There were a lot of people taking our pictures on the field—"

"Not that picture." The woman shook her head, her black hair rippling. Betha watched them remembering, reassessing. "We've heard about you ever since you came into the system over a megasec ago."

"And you didn't get from there to here in a megasec in the ship we saw." The man looked at Shadow Jack again. "You are from the Belt; maybe it's your ship. What are you, a snow pirate?"

"We're not pirating anything." Betha caught Rusty, pinned her against her suit. "We offered you a deal, this cat for a load of hydrogen. We've got nothing else that would interest you, wherever we're from. Just let us make the deal and go—"

"I'm sorry." The man looked down at the spiral of paper. "I'm afraid we *are* interested in a ship that can go from Discus . . . to the Main Belt . . . to the Demarchy . . ." Betha saw his mind work out the parameters. ". . . in one and a half megaseconds."

She wondered bleakly what he would think if he knew it had only taken a third of that. "What is it you want from us, then?" Knowing the answer, she knew now that she had failed because there had never been a way to enter Mecca undetected.

"They want your ship! Let's get out of here." Shadow Jack pushed away toward the door, pulled aside the flaps, froze. Betha turned. Facing him, in a wine-red jacket flawlessly embroidered, was the man who worked for the government. Impeccable . . . The man's eyes fixed on her in return, and on Shadow Jack. He stared, incredulous, and she knew that this time he was staring at wild, filthy hair and streaked faces. Not at her paleness—she knew from his eyes that her face held no surprises for him. "Captain Torgussen," he nodded. "And not from Lansing—obviously."

"You have the advantage of me," Betha said. "I'm afraid I've forgotten your name."

He smiled. It hardened as he turned to the Tirikis, making a bow. "And just what *does* Tiriki Distillates want with the starship?" His hand found the front of

Shadow Jack's suit, pushed him back into the room. "I guess you weren't kidding, boy, when you told us what you do for a living."

"Who are you?" the woman asked, indignant.

"Wadie Abdhiamal, representing the Demarchy government."

"Government?" The man made a face. "Then this is none of your business, Abdhiamal. Butt out before you get into trouble."

"That's monopolist talk, Tiriki. And I think you've got the ideas to go with it. I'm here on business—these people and their ship are what I came to Mecca to find. The government has claimed the ship in the name of all the people of the Demarchy."

"Your government claims don't hold air, Abdhiamal." The man glanced down at his reflection on the counter top, readjusting his soft beret. "You know you've got nothin' to back them up. We found these two first, and we're keeping them."

"Public opinion will back me up. Nobody's goin' to let Tiriki have total control of that ship. I'll call a public hearing—"

"Use my screen." The man pointed. "When we tell the people how the government has been goin' behind the Demarchy's back looking for the starship, they're not goin' to hear a word you say. You'll be out before you know what happened, and I mean out of everything."

"But you'll be out one starship—and that's all that matters to me. Set up a hearing."

The woman moved toward the wall screen.

"Just a damn minute!" Betha turned desperately, caught them all in a look. "Sixty seconds—one minute, where I come from—to mention some things you seem to have forgotten about my ship. One, it is *my* ship. And two, only I know where it is. And three, if you think you'll get it without my full cooperation, you're wrong. My crew will destroy it before they'll let it be taken—and that will destroy any ship that gets within three thousand kilometers of it." Shadow Jack came back to her side, his face questioning. The others were silent, waiting, their frustration and greed sucking at her like flames. "Now, then. You seem to have reached an impasse. But I came here to make a deal, and I'm still willing to make a deal—since I don't think I have any other choice. I doubt if you'll let us leave, in any case.

"So . . . suppose each of you tell me why you want my ship so much, and then I'll tell you who gets it. And it wouldn't hurt if you mention what's in it for me—" Rusty began to struggle, clawing for a foothold on her slick suiting. She saw Abdhiamal watch the cat, smile with irrelevant fascination before he met her gaze in turn. He didn't answer; waiting for the opposition, she thought. "Well?" She turned away, afraid of him, afraid of herself, afraid to let him see it.

The Tirikis spoke softly together. They faced her finally, beautiful and determined. "Your ship would build up our business—and revolutionize the Demarchy's trade. The way things stand we don't have all the snow we need where it's easy to get at; we have to go to the Rings, and it's a hard trip with nuclear-electric rockets. And the Ringers make it even harder, because they know we can't do anythin' that would threaten our allotments of gases. If we had your ship we wouldn't have to depend on them. Your ship would make the Demarchy a better place to live. . . . You could continue to captain it, work for us. We'll pay you well. You'll be part of the richest, most powerful company in the Demarchy—"

"And when the Demarchy objects, that company will make your ship into a superweapon and take over." Abdhiamal held her eyes.

She felt her eyelids flicker; he slipped out of focus

as she shook her head, denying. "No one will use my ship as a weapon. Not even you, Abdhiamal, if that's why you want it."

"The government wants it so it won't become a weapon and bring on a new civil war. God knows, the old one's still killin' us. Somebody's got to see that the ship is used for the good of the whole Demarchy, and not turned against us. It could be the stimulus we need to revive the whole Belt, the technology you have on board. We might be able to duplicate your ramscoop, build our own, reestablish some kind of regular communication outside the Demarchy. You could help us—"

"Don't listen to him!" the woman said. "We're the government, we, the people. He's got no authority to do anythin'. You'd be torn apart by everybody who wants your ship. He can't protect you. Stay with us. We'll take care of you." She lifted her hands. "You've got nowhere else to turn." Betha recognized the threat behind it.

"They'll take care of you, all right," Shadow Jack whispered. His gloved hand caught Betha's wrist, squeezing until it bruised, "Don't do it, Betha! They're all liars. You can't trust any of 'em."

"Shadow Jack." She turned slowly, her hand still locked in his, and touched him with her eyes. He let go; she saw the anger drain out of him, leaving his face empty. "What about the hydrogen—for Lansing?"

"We'll send them a shipment; whatever they need."

"And you?" She faced Abdhiamal again. "Is it true that your promises are worthless?"

"The government only does the Demarchy's pleasure. Why don't we ask the Demarchy? We'll call a general meeting, and let you tell them all about your ship. Tell everyone the location—but warn 'em too, to keep away—tell them what you told us. Then nobody will be at an advantage. I'll tell them what your ship could mean to all of them, to the whole Belt. Everybody will have a hand in decidin' how to make the best use of the opportunity, the way things were designed to be done. . . . The Demarchy means you no harm, Captain. But we need your help. Give it to us, and you can name your own reward."

"Anything but a ticket home." Shadow Jack searched her face; she averted her eyes.

"All right." She reached down for Rusty's carrying case, forced herself to look at Abdhiamal again. "Abdhiamal, I'll try it your way. . . ."

He smiled, and she couldn't see behind it; she fought the desire to trust him. "Thanks." He turned to the Tirikis. "Set up a meeting."

"No. Wait." Betha shook her head. "Not here. I want to be on my ship when I make the announcement. If everyone has to know where it is, some lunatic will try to take it no matter what I say. I have to be there, to countermand my orders; I don't want to lose my ship now. I'm sure you don't, either?" She looked back at him. "We'll take you to the ship; we can broadcast from there. . . . After all, it's not going to get away from you without fuel, is it?"

"I suppose not. And I suppose you're right." He nodded once, watching the Tirikis. "Okay, I'll accept your terms."

"Go with 'em, Abdhiamal." Esrom Tiriki's voice mocked him. "That'll give us plenty of time to spread the news of this; the mediamen will tear you apart. By the time you call a meetin' you'll be public enemy number one. Nobody will listen to you then. You can count on it." His hand jerked at the counter's edge, chopping down.

She saw Abdhiamal's smile tighten. "Let's get goin', then."

She pushed Rusty, protesting, into the case and

sealed the lid. She felt a small joy at a sacrifice refused, and felt the Tirikis' eyes change enviously behind her. She smiled faintly.

"How can you smile now, after that's happened?" Shadow Jack muttered. He picked up his helmet.

Softly she said, "Didn't I tell you there was always a reason to keep smiling?"

LANSING 04 AND RANGER (DEMARCHY SPACE)
+ 1.73 MEGASECONDS

Wadie watched the starship grow on the screen in the cramped, stinking cabin of the *Lansing 04*. His admiration grew with it—and his heartfelt gratitude. This was the Ship from Outside, a ship to cross interstellar space at interstellar speeds, with a body streamlined to silken grace as a protection against the corroding particulate wind. It had none of the ugly angularity of the spacecraft he had always seen; it was pragmatic perfection, and there hadn't been a ship like it in the Heaven system in generations. The prewar starships of the Heaven Belt had been converted into the deadliest of warships during the war—and had been destroyed, every one, just as the access to the basic requirements for life, the delicate balance of survival, had been destroyed. In the end the Main Belt had become a vast mausoleum, and now the isolated survivors were disappearing, like patches of melting snow....

He looked down at the back of Shadow Jack's head. His own head ached insufferably. He looked back at the screen again, counting the seconds until they reached the ship. Even if it hadn't been all he imagined, still it would have been a haven, an escape from the past two hundred kilosecs of suffocating indignity in the foulness of this scrap-metal coffin. And an escape from the sullen, hostile boy and the small, blunt woman who might as well have been a man, like all the other women who pushed their way out into space. He watched her as she soothed the cat above the humming control board, the rings shining on her hands. He looked down at the silver-and-ruby ring on his own thumb, the gift of that other spacing woman and her man, and wondered wearily why this one bothered to wear so many rings, when she obviously wasn't interested in her appearance.

The starship's image blotted out the stars; unobtrusively, he used his water ration to clean his face and hands.

Not a ship. Wadie pulled back, halfway through the *Ranger*'s lock, as the room opened before him. *This is a world.*

"This is the control room." The captain moved past him, her voice husky in her hoarse throat; he heard the clanking as Shadow Jack still fumbled with a pressure suit in the lock behind him. He drew a long breath of cool air, coughed once as his startled lungs reacted.

"Hello, Pappy."

The captain pushed off from the wall, with the indefinable lack of grace that marked her alienness more than her face and hair. She moved across the vastness of the control room toward the instrument panels. He suddenly realized that the room was not empty, that he was being studied by a girl and a short pale-skinned man. "Betha–" A smile spread in the man's grizzled beard–an old man, too old to still be in space, to still be sound. . . . The slim brown girl wasn't looking at him at all, but only staring through him toward the lock. She was a Belter, ludicrously dressed in faded pants cinched by a flapping belt.

"You mean to tell me this is all you brought back?"

The old man gestured at him, half joking, half appalled. "This—fop? You traded our Rusty for *this*?"

The captain shook her head, amused, said blithely, "No, not 'Shadow Jack and the Beanstalk,' Pappy. I just said we didn't get the golden goose . . . and maybe we've been the golden goose, all along, and didn't know it."

Wadie felt Shadow Jack brush by him with the cat in his arms. The boy tossed her out into the air, giving her momentum, and she paddled on across the room, perfectly at ease.

"Rusty!"

She made rusty meows of pleasure, moving toward the old man's familiar hands.

The Belter girl's face startled him, transformed by wild bliss as her eyes found Shadow Jack. He looked away from her, back at the old man. "Wadie Abdhiamal, representin' the Demarchy. And usually better than this. I'm afraid two hundred kilosecs in that deathtrap didn't do much for my appearance." The old man laughed.

Shadow Jack glanced back at him. "Try it for a couple megasecs, sometime."

The captain drifted against the control panel, lines of strain settling on her face again, making it grim. "It was hell, Pappy. I didn't want to make you come into Demarchy space to pick us up, but I don't know how much longer the life-support system would have held up. It wasn't adequate for two—and with three . . ." She rubbed her face, smearing grime. "The past two days were worse than the whole two weeks going in. But we had to bring him along. It was the only way we could get out of there. Their communications network is incredible; they already knew everything about us—everyone did, on every single separate piece of rock. And every one of them just waiting to grab our ship and play God with it—just like the Ringers.

We can't trust either of them now; if we want hydrogen we're going to have to take it."

"Captain Torgussen," Wadie said, "the government only wants—"

"I know what you want, Abdhiamal. My ship. You made it clear enough. But your Demarchy will have to catch us first." Her eyes cut him, blue glass. "I'm sorry, Abdhiamal, but you're on our ground now. Consider yourself our hostage."

Shadow Jack laughed, sitting back in the air. The girl moved away from the panel to his side, her face expressionless.

Wadie said nothing, saw the captain hesitate.

"You don't seem very surprised. You didn't believe what I told you at Mecca, and still you let this happen?"

"I didn't know whether to believe you or not. After what you've been through, I figured maybe you really had given orders for the destruction of your ship, and I didn't want to take that chance. And I didn't want to take any chances with the Tirikis. And if you were lying about cooperating . . . well, I'm on your ship; that give me another chance to change your mind. Heaven Belt needs your help."

"We don't owe you anything; greed and hostility are all we've met in Heaven Belt."

"Why did you come here in the first place, except to trade on the fact that you figured we were ridin' high? Why shouldn't we be as greedy? One hundred million people—most of the Main Belt—died in the first hundred megasecs after the war. And the ones that are left . . ." He pointed at Shadow Jack and the girl. "Look at Lansing. Their people won't last another circuit around Heaven. And we're all headed for the same thing, unless we have your ship."

She frowned, hooked a shoe under the security rail that edged the panel. "The fact remains that we have rights of our own, as human beings—including the right to leave this system if we choose—and you're not willing to give them to us. It's true we came here to trade, because we thought Heaven had things we wanted. But you've got nothing to offer, and we can't afford to waste our ship and the rest of our lives for nothing. Morningside can't afford it. We just don't have the resources to throw away on you."

"I—admit we didn't consider your position—" He broke off, the crassness of it embarrassing him. "We made a mistake, not considerin' your position. It was a stupid mistake. But we aren't the Ringers; we don't just want your ship, we want your cooperation. We might still have some things you'd want. It wouldn't have to be forever. The use of your ship, its reactor, and its shop, for a hundred and fifty megasecs. We'll deal with you fairly." The part of him that had questioned MacWong asked, *Will we?* The Belter kids stared at him, distrustful, more in sympathy with outsiders than with a man from their own system.

The captain moved restlessly. "I don't believe that. Everything I've seen shows me I can't depend on the Demarchy. You can't even depend on each other. Even if you meant every word you said, someone else would make it a lie and attack us. . . . I'm not blind, Abdhiamal, I can see what's happened here, and I know it's true that you need help. If I'd only had some sign to prove to me that at least the Demarchy was worthy of our trust. But I haven't. We can't help you; you won't let us. It's impossible."

"Captain, I—"

"The matter is closed." Something in her voice told him that it was closed, irrevocably, and that the reason went much deeper than a simple betrayal of trust.

Not understanding, he only nodded, his own fatigue and exasperation leaving him defeated. "To what end am I your hostage then, Captain?"

Her eyes shifted, clouding. "I don't know. Whatever end we come to, for better or worse . . . will be yours too, I suppose. You helped us out of a tight spot, Abdhiamal. Inadvertently, but you did help us. I'll try to be as fair to you. If we get the hydrogen we need, I'll find a way to get you back to the Demarchy before we leave the system. It will only be a—temporary inconvenience." She looked at him strangely for a moment; turning away, she reached for the old man's arm. "Oh, Christ, Pappy, I'm so tired. So glad to be back." He pulled her close, too close; held her until she broke away, kissing him once, tenderly.

Old enough to be her father . . . surprise let a grimace of distaste pull his own mouth down; he covered it as they looked back at him. Only four, in this large, empty room; and two of them were Belters. Too empty. "Where's the rest of your crew?"

The old man glanced at the captain; she shook her head. "It doesn't matter; he'll find it out soon enough, I suppose." Her hand gestured at the screen and knotted into a fist. "They all died at Discus. And we're going back. Pappy, get started on a course for Discus. We can't risk staying here any longer. We're going to take what we need from the Ringers, Abdhiamal, any way we can, and that's going to suit me fine." She threw it at him, defiant, before she turned to Shadow Jack and the girl. "I'm going to get us out of here as fast as I can. I want to be sure no one from the Demarchy can touch us. We'll be doing one gee for five or six days, again, to get us back to the Rings."

"It'll be worth it." Shadow Jack cracked his knuckles. The girl's mouth set in a line; she nodded. She moved closer to Shadow Jack, stroking his bare arm lightly. He glanced down at her hand, irritated, but didn't pull away.

"Thirsty?" she said. He straightened out of his drifting slouch, smiled suddenly, wiping his hand across his mouth. "Yeah!" He pushed off from the wall and they left the room.

The old man was strapped into a seat, working at the panel. The captain moved out into the air to collect a pencil and an unidentifiable metal cube. She pushed the cat into a compartment in the wall.

"Captain—"

She started back toward the control board. "What?"

"I'd like permission to use your radio."

"Refused." She reached a chair, maneuvered herself down.

"But I need to—"

"Refused." She turned her back, cutting him off as she began her work at the board. He waited, studying the tasteless combination of pale-blue walls and green carpet. He noticed a stripe of deeper blue on the wall, an arrow, and the word DOWN.

"The Lansing ship is secure. Are the co-ords in, Pappy?"

"They're in. Ready when you are."

"Right. Ignition . . . thirty seconds. Feet on the ground, all of you!" The last of it went over an intercom, rattling off of walls through the empty heart of the ship. Wadie watched her hands move through a sequence on the panel, felt the light, familiar hand of gravity settle on his shoulders. And begin to bear down: His feet touched the floor, the drag against his legs continued, increasing past the point of familiarity, past the point of comfort. He backed up, caught hold of a bar along the wall, remembering thirty seconds of one gee on a Ringer ship, and realizing what it would be like for the next five hundred thousand seconds. Pain wrenched his muscles; the blue-on-blue streaked wall filled his vision DOWN. . . . His hands tightened, and he stood, enduring the pain, ignoring the heart that beat against his ribs like a fist.

He stood—and moved tentatively away from the wall, as the pressure bearing down on him stabilized. Dizziness made him sway, but he controlled it, balanced precariously as the captain and the old man rose from their seats. They looked toward him with expectant pity; the cat struggled out of the wall through a plastic porthole, made a circuit of his legs, licked his booted foot consolingly with her tongue. He folded his arms; looked down, and back at them across the room. He smiled, blandly.

The captain turned and walked out of the room. The cat bounded after her, tail flying like a banner.

"Abdhiamal, is it?" The old man came over to him, held out a hand. "My name's Welkin, navigator on the *Ranger*."

Wadie nodded, shook his hand, wondered at his motive in offering it. He noticed that Welkin's hand was bright with golden rings, like Betha Torgussen's; and that his grip was strong and firm. . . . But the old man must be tough, if he could take one gee—ten meters per second squared, the gravity of Old Earth. This was what it had been like to live on Earth. A crash and Shadow Jack's pained "Hell!" rose from somewhere below them. *No wonder we called this system Heaven.*

RANGER (IN TRANSIT, DEMARCHY TO DISCUS) +2.25 MEGASECONDS

Fifty kiloseconds later Wadie climbed the empty stairwell, one step and then another—wanting to crawl and knowing there was no one to see it, but determined that he would keep control over something, if only his own dignity. He had investigated the lower levels of the ship's living area: the crew's quarters; the alien lushness of a hydroponics lab adapted to one gravity; the workshop—the last memory was almost a hunger. He had seen everything but the section on the second level, behind a sealed doorway where a warning light blinked red. And everywhere he had been stunned by the incredible waste—of water, of air, of living space—in a matrix of drab austerity that was primitive compared to the Demarchy's sophistication. He contemplated the irony in the idea that the Morningsiders considered themselves poor, when in some ways they were the richest people he had ever seen.

He reached the top of the stairs, leaned against the railing until his dizziness passed and his heartbeat slowed. His muscles ached dully when he stood, and when he moved pain burned in his trembling legs like a hot wire. He did his best to put his new clothes in order before he entered the control room.

The others were already there, watching something on the viewscreen. The captain and Welkin sat in chairs. Shadow Jack and the girl lay on the carpet, spreading their weight over the greatest area. The girl was trying to do pushups, her body rigid from the knees, as he looked in. He saw her elbows tremble, watched her collapse face down on the cushion. She lay spread-eagled on the floor, defeated. "I can't."

"Then don't," Shadow Jack said, and more gently, "It'll be over soon, Bird Alyn; we don't have to get used to it." He flipped playing cards out into the air, watching their incredibly swift plummet to the rug. "Look who finally woke up." He looked back over his shoulder; the cat sidled past his head and sat down on the cards.

Wadie bowed casually, carefully keeping his balance. No one moved in return, and indignation rose in him until he remembered that he couldn't expect civility here. Pirates . . . He almost smiled, struck by the memory of what it had meant to be called a Belter, once, in the time when the only Asteroid Belt was Sol's. He studied the captain's face, clean now like her fair cropped hair; met something in her eyes that startled him. She glanced down, lighting a pipe. The tangy sweetness of whatever burned stirred memories in him, instinctive, of things he had never seen.

"At least you're a likelier-looking trade this time," Welkin said.

Wadie looked down at the blue cotton work shirt, the blue denim pants that stopped ten centimeters short of his ankles. He had forced the pants neatly into his polished boots. The boots braced his legs, but weighted them down like lead. "At least I'm clean." He stepped carefully over the doorsill and crossed the room, holding his head up, back straight. He reached the nearest swivel seat and lowered himself into it, leaned back easily, breathing again. The girl stared up at him, awed. Shadow Jack looked away with a frown; he muttered and pushed the cat, scattering cards.

"Captain . . ." Wadie turned in his seat, reordering his arguments. He stopped, as he realized what they had been watching on the screen. "You've been monitoring Demarchy communications?" Six separate images showed on the bright screen, each one a different broadcast frequency. He recognized a general newscast, three corporation hypes, two local arbitration debates.

The captain nodded. "It's been—enlightening."

"Has there been anything about your ship from the Tirikis?"

"Yes, news items; and there was a—" She glanced back at the screen, as two of the broadcast segments suddenly disappeared, replaced by an octagonal star caught in a golden paisley, on a field of black. As they watched, the symbol blotted out the rest of the segments one by one. "What is this, Abdhiamal?"

"It's a call for a general meeting; any demarch who wants to participate can monitor the final debate, startin' now, and vote on the issues involved." He remembered uneasily that it had been two hundred and fifty kiloseconds since they had left Mecca, more than two hundred and fifty kilosecs since his last report. "I expect this'll be the debate about your ship, and what happened at Mecca. The Tirikis started to promo the second we left the rock; and nobody's heard a word from me. I'd like to monitor the debate. And I'd like a chance to defend myself, if you'll give me an open channel."

She put her pipe aside. "All right, I'll monitor the meeting. You can listen; but I can't let you speak."

"Why not? Your ship's clear. And they can track you by your exhaust, they don't need a radio fix—"

"I don't need you telling them our plans. I'd rather let them guess."

"Captain, I need to talk to them. This meetin' could mean my job." They all looked at him, unresponsive. He swallowed his irritation. "You—experienced the communications network we've got; it's from before the war, and it still works as it should. It's what makes the Demarchy work—every demarch's got equal priority on it, and anybody with a gripe about anythin' can broadcast it. Everybody who's involved or interested can debate. If they need to, they take a general vote, and the vote is law."

"Mob rule?" Welkin said. "The tyranny of the majority."

"No." He gestured at the slender golden teardrop on the screen, symbol of the hundred-and-forty-million-kilometer teardrop distribution of the trojan asteroids. "Not here. You can't get a mob together across millions of kilometers of space. It keeps the voters' self-interest confined to their own rock. They're independent as hell, and they're informed, and they judge. A jury of peers."

"Then why would you be worried about losing your job?"

"Because I'm not there to defend myself; the Tirikis can claim anything, and if nobody hears different from me, what are they goin' to think, except that it's true? My boss will be answering them in my place, and he doesn't even know what's happened. If I can't tell them, I could take him down with me. The government floats on water, and if you rock the boat you drown."

The captain leaned forward, pressing her hands together. "I'm sorry, Abdhiamal, but you should have considered that before you came with me. I can't afford to let you speak now. . . . Do you still want to listen in?"

He nodded. All the symbols but one were gone from the screen again; as he watched, the time lag closed and the last one faded. The general meeting had begun.

". . . should already have put our fusion craft in pursuit." Wadie rested his neck against the seatback, as Lije MacWong's final argument drew to a close on the screen. "We've done all we can to follow the wishes of the Demarchy. Too many things are still unclear to us, too, because we only know what you do. I'm a civil servant, no more, no less. If the people want to remove me for working in the people's interest, that's your privilege. But I don't feel that I've done anything to betray your trust." A band of color showed at the bottom of the screen, slowly turning violet from blue; voter participation was eighty per cent and rising.

Wadie watched the manicured brown hands fold on the gargoyled desk top, the pale compelling eyes that had challenged the Demarchy before and won. They disappeared suddenly; the seconds passed. REBUTTAL: ESROMTIRIKI flashed on the screen. He felt his mouth tighten as Tiriki's serene, golden face appeared, eyes gleaming like metal. "The fact remains that the government . . ."

The captain leaned back in her seat, fingers tapping soundlessly on the chair arms. "He's one of the trolls, Pappy. Handsome, isn't he?" She looked up. "And out for our blood. How does it go again? 'I smell the blood of an Englishman. Be he alive, or be he dead—' " She broke off, took a deep breath. "Screw Jack and the Beanstalk. . . . What was that about fusion ships, Abdhiamal? I thought you said the Demarchy depended on fission power and fission-powered electric rockets?"

He nodded. "We have three small fusion craft left from before the war; they're our navy, if you want to call it that. But you've got a big lead on them. They couldn't catch you before you got to Discus."

"But it could give us less time to maneuver once we're there."

". . . the government agent Abdhiamal threatened us and kidnapped the Outsiders who had come to us to negotiate. Two hundred kilosecs have passed without any further word from him. Their knowledge would have benefited the entire Demarchy, it could have saved Heaven—but because of this 'government man' we've lost the crew and the starship forever. Consider that, when you make your final decision." The band of light below him showed an ever-deepening violet.

Wadie's hands tightened over nothing. FINAL REBUTTAL: LIJE MACWONG showed on the screen.

"I regret to say that, in honesty, I can't deny Demarch Tiriki's final accusation. Wadie Abdhiamal, a negotiator from my agency, has overstepped his authority to a degree I consider criminal. He has in the past been suspect of questionable loyalty, of known Ringer sympathies, and I frankly consider it possible that he intends to aid them in usin' that ship against us. I can only repeat that he was acting without my consent, or the consent of any other person in the government. This agency isn't, and never was, a party to these actions. He alone committed a crime, and like any other criminal, he should be found guilty . . ."

Wadie straightened, felt something grate in his neck.

". . . of treason against the Demarchy . . ."

"Lije!" he whispered, incredulous, willing the mahogany face to turn and the pale eyes to meet his own.

". . . and so, fellow demarchs, I want you to reconsider the basic issue before you make your decision. This should not be a simple vote of no confidence against a government that's served you well; this is a judgment on the fate of the one man who has betrayed the hopes of us all. I ask instead for a bill of attainder against Wadie Abdhiamal, government negotiator, for treason . . ."

You bastard— He pushed himself up and moved through a nightmare to the panel.

". . . let him never set foot on any territory of the Demarchy on pain of death. He has betrayed us all . . ."

"Let me talk." He reached toward the banks of buttons.

The captain caught his arm. "No."

". . . I further urge again that all fusion-powered vessels be impressed into the pursuit of the alien ship; we must prevent it from reachin' our enemies. We must have that ship for ourselves!"

PROPOSITION flashed on the screen. BILL OF ATTAINDER AGAINST WADIE ABDHIAMAL, NEGOTIATOR. CHARGES: TREASON. PENALTY: DEATH. NEGATING PREVIOUS CHARGE: GOVERNMENT NEGLIGENCE.

He stepped back from the panel, his fingers twitching uselessly; his hand dropped. He went to his seat, sat down heavily, watching the ballots begin to register, APPROVE, OBJECT, numbers tallying with the passing seconds. Below them the percentage-of-voters band moved through red into orange into yellow. Five hundred seconds until it would reach full violet . . . five hundred seconds for the last votes to record from the outermost rocks of the trojans. An insignificant time lag, by the standards of the prewar Belt, as one hundred and forty million kilometers was an insignificant distance. Their closeness had meant survival for the trojans after the war; it meant death for him, now, letting men vote without hesitation, without reflection. He waited. The others waited with him, saying nothing. The ship's drive filled the silence with vibration, almost sound, almost intruding, the only constant in the sudden chaos of the universe.

PROPOSITION APPROVED. They found him guilty,

twenty to one, and sentenced him to die. He watched the death order repeat and merge, like a thing already forgotten, into a new cycle of debate over the use of fusion ships. He raised his leaden hands, let them drop again, smiled, looking back at the others. "Now I finally know how MacWong's kept his job for so long."

The captain cut off the debate, filling the screen with the void of his future.

"I guess I see the distinction between 'demarchy' and plain 'democracy,' " Welkin said quietly.

"Welkin, you don't have the right to make any moral judgments about Heaven Belt."

"He's got the right," Shadow Jack said. He sat up, pulling his feet forward. "The crew of this ship, they were . . ." He fumbled for words. "They were all married, they were a family; all of them together. And they all died in the Rings, except . . ." He glanced at Welkin and Betha Torgussen, back at Wadie, and down, twisting his fingers. "They all died."

Wadie watched the captain, her arm resting on the old man's shoulder. "I'm not married," he said, his voice flat. "And now I never will be." She looked back at him, not understanding, useless apology in her eyes, and a surprising sorrow. He got up, resenting the intrusion of her unexpected, and undesired, sympathy. "Well, Captain, you've ruined your final opportunity for a constructive agreement with the Demarchy. For my sake, I hope you have better luck with the Ringers than you did the last time." He went out of the room and down the spiraling stairs. No one followed.

RANGER (IN TRANSIT, DEMARCHY TO DISCUS) + 2.40 MEGASECONDS

Betha sat alone at the control panel in the soothing semidarkness, gazing at the endless bright stream of Demarchy television traffic, soundless by her own choice, that still trailed after them, two hundred million kilometers out. Caught in a spell of hypnotic revulsion, she marveled at the perpetual motion of the Demarchy media machine, wondered how any citizen—demarch?—ever made a sane decision under the constant dinning of a hundred different distortions of the truth. And remembering the mediamen on the field at Mecca, she should have known enough to believe Wadie Abdhiamal and let him speak....

She cut off the broadcasts abruptly and put the crescent of Discus on the screen. She saw the *Ranger* in her mind, an infinitesimal mote, alone in the five hundred million kilometers of barren darkness, tracing back along Discus's path around the sun from the isolate swarm of rocks that was the Demarchy. She remembered then that they were not entirely alone. Expanding her mind's vision, she saw the Demarchy's grotesque, ponderous freighters loaded with ores or volatiles, crawling across the desolation; ships that took a hundred days to cross what the *Ranger* crossed in six. It was a barely bridgeable gap, now; and the survival of the Demarchy, and the Rings, depended on it. And someday there would be no ships....

But now, tracing the violet mist of the *Ranger*'s exhaust, she saw what might be three fusion craft, barely registering on the ship's most sensitve instruments.

She cursed the Demarchy, the obsessive veneer of sophistication, the artificial gaiety, the pointless waste of their media broadcasts. Fools, reveling in their fanatical independence when they should all be working together; living on self-serving self-sufficiency, with no stable government to control them, no honest bonds of kinship, but only the equal selffishness of every other citizen. . . . And their women; useless, frivolous, gaudy, the ultimate waste in a society that desperately needed every resource, including its human resources.

Fragments of conversation drew together in her mind, and she remembered suddenly what Clewell had said about crippled Bird Alyn. Perhaps in a sense they were a resource, sound and fertile women who had to be protected, in a society where radiation levels were always abnormally high; women who had let the protection grow into a way of life as artificial as everything else in their world. . . . Perhaps the danger of genetic damage lay at the root of all the incomprehensible involutions of their sexual mores. Desperate people did desperate things; even the people of Morningside, in the beginning. . . .

She turned slightly in her seat, to glance at Shadow Jack lying asleep on the floor, lost in a peaceful dream, a book of Morningside landscapes open beside him. She wondered, if those were desperate measures for the Demarchy, what must be true for Lansing. Her hand met on the panel, caressing her rings, as Wadie Abdhiamal entered the room.

"Captain." He made the requisite bow. She nodded in return, watching him cross the room: the proper demarch, compulsively polite, compulsively immaculate. And as awkward as a child taking his first steps, moving in one gravity. His face looked haggard, showing the effects of stress and fluid loss. She remembered seeing him use his drinking water to wash his face on the *Lansing 04*, thinking that no one noticed. . . . She brushed absently at her own hair. "Have you found everything you've needed, Abdhiamal? Have you eaten?" He had not joined the rest of them when they ate together in the dining hall.

He sat down. "Yes . . . somethin'. I don't know what." He looked vaguely ill, remembering. "I'm afraid I don't get along well with meat."

"How—are you feeling?"

"Homesick." He laughed, self-deprecatingly, as if it were a lie. He gazed at the empty screen. Rusty materialized on his knee, settled into his lap, tail muffling her nose. He stroked her back with a dark, meticulous hand; Betha noticed the massive silver ring on his thumb, inlaid with rubies.

"I'm sorry." She pulled her pipe out of the hip pocket of her jeans, quieting her hands with its carven familiarity.

"Don't be." He shifted and Rusty muttered querulously, tail flicking. "Because you were right, Captain; and I made the right choice in comin' with you. The Demarchy can't be allowed to take your ship; nobody in Heaven Belt can. . . . I'm not saying that because of what happened to me—" Something in his voice told her that was not entirely true. "I've known all along, from the first time I heard about this ship, that it would make too many people want to play God." He looked up. "Even if it's not my right, I'd still turn your ship over to the Demarchy if I had the chance—if I thought it'd save them. But it wouldn't. The government *is* too weak, they'd never be able to keep an equilibrium now." His fingers dug into the soft arms of the chair; his face was expressionless. "So I'll tell you this. I'll help you get out of here, however I can.

Anythin' I can do, anythin' you want to know. As my final service to the Demarchy: to buy them a little more time and save them from themselves." His eyes went to Discus on the screen. "If I've got to be a traitor, I'll be a good one. I take pride in my work."

She broke away from tracing his every movement, her face hot. "If you really mean that, Abdhiamal . . . I want your help, whatever your personal motives. I need to know anything you can tell me about the Ringers—especially I need the number and the locations of their distilleries. No matter how primitive they are, it's going to take careful planning to steal anything from them with an unarmed starship. . . . And as you say, I haven't done very well so far at getting what I want. Strategy was always Eric's—was never my strong point."

"On the contrary. You outnegotiated us all, at Mecca." Irony acknowledged her with a smile. "I expect I can give you reasonably accurate coordinates; I spent a lot of time in the Rings about two hundred and fifty megasecs ago, when we helped 'em enlarge their main distillery. As a matter of fact, I—" He broke off abruptly. "Tell me something about Morningside, Captain. Tell me about the way your people get things done. You don't seem to approve of our way."

She studied the words, trying to find the reason behind his change of subject; certain only that he didn't really want an answer but simply a distraction. *And so do I.* "No, I can't say that I do approve, Abdhiamal. But that's the Demarchy's business, except when it gets in my way. . . . I guess that you could say we emphasize our kinship—as fellow human beings, but especially as blood relatives. You already know about our multiple-marriage family unit." She glanced up, away; his eyes made no comment, but she sensed his uneasiness. "Above it is our 'clan'—not in the Old

World technical sense, except that it tells you who you can't marry—your particular parent-family, your sibs, your own children. All your relations stretch out beyond it . . . almost to infinity, sometimes. We all try to take care of our own; everybody on Morningside has relations somewhere. . . . Except that a person who isn't willing to share the work finds that even his own relations aren't glad to share the rewards forever.

"The only formalized social structure above the clan level is what we call a 'moiety' . . ." She lost the sound of her own voice, and even the aching awareness of Abdhiamal's presence, in vivid memories that filled the spaces between her words with sudden yearning. Borealis moiety: an arbitrary economic unit for the distribution of goods and services. Borealis moiety: her home, her job, her family, her world . . . a laughing child—her daughter, or herself—falling back to make angel imprints in a bank of snow. . . .

"Our industries are independently run, as yours are—but I suppose you'd call them 'monopolistic.' They cooperate, not for profits, but because they have to, or they'd fail. It works because we never have enough of anything, especially people. My parent family and a lot of my close relatives run a tree farm in the Borealis moiety . . . my wife Claire worked there too. Some families specialize in a trade, but Clewell and I and our spouses were a little of everything. . . ." She remembered day's end in the endless twilight, the family sitting down together at the long dark wood table, while their children served them dinner. The soothing warmth of the fire, the sunset that never faded from the skylight of a semisubterranean house. The small talk of the day's small triumphs, the comfortable fatigue . . . the welcome homecoming of a spouse whose job had kept him or her away for days or sometimes weeks. Eric, returning from the arbitration of a long-drawn dispute—

She saw Wadie Abdhiamal, sitting back in his chair in the control room of the *Ranger*. A negotiator . . . *I settle disputes, work out trade agreements. . . .* Abdhiamal looked back at her with a faintly puzzled expression. She shook her head. *Stop it. Stop being a fool!* "I . . . I almost forgot—we have a High Council, too. It's a kind of parliament, made up of ombudsmen from the various moieties, elected to terms of service. It deals with what little interplanetary trade we manage and the emergency shipments. It originated the proposal for our trip to Heaven. It doesn't have much to do with our daily lives—"

"Then in a way you are like us," Abdhiamal said, "without a strong centralized government, with emphasis on independence—"

"No." She shook her head again, denying more than the words. "We're like a family. We get things done through cooperation, not competition, the way the Demarchy does. Your system is a paradox: the individual has absolute control, and yet no control at all, if they don't fit in with the majority. We cooperate and compromise because we know we all need each other just to survive. . . . And considering the position the Demarchy is in right now, I'd say it can hardly afford to go on putting self-interest above everything else, either."

Abdhiamal blinked, as if her words had struck him in the face. But he only shrugged. "Needless to say, we don't see ourselves in quite that light. I suppose your idea of cooperation is closer to the Ringers' Grand Harmony." There was no scarcasm in it. "They emphasize copperation above all too, because they have to; they weren't as fortunate as the Demarchy, after the war. But they have a socialist state and a strong navy; they get cooperation at the point of a gun. And that's no cooperation at all, really; that's why they're anathema, as far as the Demarchy's concerned. They don't trust individual human nature, even it if is backed up by family ties."

Betha struggled against a sudden irrational resentment. "It's worked well enough so far. But then we don't kill any stranger who comes to us in need, either."

"Maybe you just never had a good enough reason, Captain."

She stiffened. Apology showed instantly on his face and behind it, she saw a reflection of her own disorientation, the frustration of a stranger trapped in an alien universe. He was a man with no family . . . and now no friends, no world, no future. And she suspected that he was not a man who was used to making mistakes—or used to sharing a burden, or sharing a life . . . *not Eric.*

"I'm sorry, Captain. Please accept my apologies." Abdhiamal hesitated. "And—let me apologize for my tactlessness after the general meeting, as well."

"I understand." She saw annoyance begin behind his eyes; stood up, not seeing it change into a kind of need. "If you'll excuse me . . ." She moved away, reaching for an excuse, an escape. "I—I have to see Clewell, down in the shop."

"You mind if I go with you?" His voice surprised her.

She hesitated, halfway across the room. "Well, I . . . no, why should I?"

He rose, setting Rusty down. The cat leaped away, rumpled, moved across the room to where Shadow Jack still lay asleep, his face buried now in the pillow. Rusty settled on the softness beside his head, one speckled paw stretched protectively over his curled fingers.

"Poor Rusty." Betha glanced down. "She's been so lonely since . . . She was used to a lot of attention."

"She would have had all she wanted at Mecca."

"She would have been worshipped. It isn't the same."

She went down one level on the spiraling stairway, waited for him on the landing. He took each step with dignified deliberateness, his knees nearly buckling and his hand on the railing in a death grip. He stopped with studied nonchalance beside her, peering down over the polished wood banister; the well dropped four more stories, piercing the hollow needle of the ship's hull. The concentric circles of a service hatch lay pooled at the bottom.

"It's good exercise." Betha stood against the wall, avoiding the sight of the drop.

He drew back with an innocuous smile. The doorway in the wall behind him was sealed shut, the red light flashing, throwing their shadows out into the pit. "What's behind this?" His hand brushed the door's icy surface.

"That was the dayroom. That's where everyone died when we took the damage to our hull. It's not pressurized; please don't touch anything." She turned away from him, looking down at her hands. She went on down the stairs, leaving him behind.

She reached the machine shop on the fourth level, heard the rasp of a handsaw. "Pappy!" She shouted, heard the echoes rattle around the hollow torus of the shop.

"Here, Betha!"

She traced the answering echoes, began to walk, the gum soles of her shoes squeaking faintly on the wood. The irregular clack of Abdhiamal's polished boots closed with her; she didn't look at him.

"Jesus, Pappy, why in the world don't you use the cutters to do that?"

Clewell looked up as they approached, on up at the nest of lasers above the work table. "Because it's a hobby."

"Which means you stand there for hours, breaking your back to do something you could punch in and get done in a minute."

"The impatience of youth." He leaned on the saw and the end split off the wooden block and dropped. "Finished." His hand rose to his chest; seeing her watching, he lifted it further to rub his neck.

"Smartass." She looked pained, hands on hips. "I—uh, I thought you were going to check over my estimates on patching that hole in our hull?"

"I did that too. They look good to me. But we can't do anything about it now, while we're at one gee." He looked at her oddly.

Abdhiamal stooped to pick up the splintered end of the block, rubbed its roughness. oblivious. "Say, what is this stuff? It's fibrous."

"It's wood. Organic. From the trunks of trees," Clewell said. "False-oak, to be exact. It's hard, but it whittles well."

"The floor, too? All plant fibers—wood?"

He nodded. "It's easier than turning it into plastic. False-oak grows two centimeters a day out by the Boreal Sea."

Abdhiamal's hand caressed the etched metal of the tabletop; he glanced up at the cutters and the suspended protective shield. "Lasers?" His hand closed, empty, as he searched the room, loosened to point at the wide doors cut into the hull, opening directly onto space . . . at the electromagnets set into the ceiling. She saw him answering his own unspoken questions. "And what's this equipment for, over here?"

Betha followed his hand, seeing in her mind red-haired Sean at work, dauntlessly clumsy; Nikolai patiently guiding. She looked away. "Repairing microcircuits on our electronics equipment."

"You have your own fusion power plant . . . you

really could reproduce any part of this ship right here, couldn't you?"

"Theoretically. There are some I wouldn't want to try. This was a long trip; we had to be prepared for anything." *Except this.*

"God! If Park and Osuna could only see this place."

"Who?" Clewell removed the wood from a clamp.

"They're 'engineers.' " Scorn lacerated the word.

"And what's wrong with engineers?" Bethe folded her arms tightly against her stomach, raising her eyebrows.

"What's right with 'em?" Abdhiamal made an odd gesture. "They're a bunch of cannibals. They put patches on patches, tear one thing apart and use the pieces to hold three more together, and then they tear apart one of those—"

"That sounds resourceful to me."

"But they gloat about it! They think it's creation, but it's destruction. If they'd only *read* something, if only they had any imagination at all, they'd know what real creation is. The thing we could do, once . . . nobody did them better. But that's like askin' for life in a vacuum."

"Or maybe you've just got your priorities wrong, Abdhiamal! What should they do, torture themselves over the past because relics are all they have left to work with? At least they're doing something for their people, not living at the expense of everyone else like some damned fop!" Betha jerked the piece of wood out of his hands, felt splinters cut her palm. She turned her back on his surprise, strode away through her echoing anger toward the door.

* * *

Clewell smiled at Abdhiamal's astonished face. "Abdhiamal, you just told it all to an engineer."

Abdhiamal winced. "I should never have gotten out of bed . . . two megaseconds ago." He stared out into the vastness of the empty room. "I always seem to say the wrong thing to . . . your wife. I thought she was a pilot."

Clewell listened to Betha's footsteps fade as she climbed the stairs. He wondered what fresh burden she had brought with her from Mecca—that showed in her eyes and her every action, and that she could not share even with him. "She was an engineer on Morningside, before she was chosen to captain the *Ranger.* Parts of this ship are her design; she worked on its drive unit." He saw surprise again in Abdhiamal's tawny eyes. "It's the first starship we've had the resources to build since before the Low."

"Low?"

"Famine . . . emergency." Memories of past hardship and suffering rose in him too easily, drawn by the fresh memory of loss. A bruising weariness made him settle against the table's edge. He set aside the wood; morbidly picturing his own body as ancient wood, storm-battered, decaying. He sighed. "On Morningside small changes in solar activity, perturbations in our orbit, can mean disaster. When I was a boy—in the last quarter of my tenth year—we went into a 'hot spell' . . ." He saw the darkside ice sheet withdrawing, shattered bergs clogging the waters of the Boreal Sea. The sea itself had risen half a meter, flooding vital coastal industries; the crops had rotted in the fields from too much rainfall. He had watched one of his fathers kill a litter of kittens because they had nothing to feed them. And he had cried, even though his own empty stomach ached with need. *Still, after all these years* . . . "It took years for the climate to stabilize, most of my lifetime before our own lives got back to 'normal.' We've entered a High, right now, and Uhuru's stabilized—they're our closest neighbor; this flight was planned to send them aid, originally. That's why we took a chance on risking the *Ranger* to come here to Heaven." He felt the cutting edge of wind over snow on the darkside glacier, where the sky glittered with stars like splintered ice. "That's why we can't afford to stay here. Even if we go back to Morningside empty-handed, at least they'll have the ship."

Abdhiamal nodded. "I see. I told—your wife, Captain Torgussen, that I'm willing to do all I can to help you get back to Morningside—for Heaven's own good. The way things seem to be goin', your remaining here is goin' to tear Heaven apart, not pull it back together again. . . ." For a moment Clewell was reminded of someone, but the image slipped away.

He considered Abdhiamal's words, surprised—more surprised to find that he believed them. *Have we found an honest man?*

"Together we find courage,
Our song will never cease. . . ."

"What's that?" Abdhiamal said.

"Bird Alyn." Clewell heard the faint, halting music rise from the hydroponics lab. "Betha taught her some chords on the guitar; I taught her a few more songs, while we were—waiting." He heard Bird Alyn strike a sour note as she strummed. "I don't know if Claire would have approved, but the plants seem to appreciate her sincerity." He smiled. "It's not what you sing. or how, but how the singing makes you feel."

Abdhiamal smiled politely. His glance touched the scarred surface of the table, the floor, searched the room again; the smile grew taut. "You know, I sometimes have the strange feeling that I'm livin' in a dream; that somehow I've forgotten how to wake myself up." A trace of desperation edged into his voice.

"Bird Alyn said the same thing to me. Except that I think she meant it."

"Comin' from the Main Belt, she probably did. . . . Maybe I do too." Abdhiamal cleared his throat, and oddly embarrassed sound. "Welkin, I'd like to ask you a personal question. If you don't mind."

Clewell laughed. "At my age I don't have much to hide. Go ahead."

Abdhiamal paused. "Do you find it—hard to take orders from your wife?"

Clewell straightened away from the table. "Why should that make a difference to me?"

Abdhiamal looked at him strangely. "Frankly I never met a woman I'd trust to make my decisions for me."

Clewell remembered what he had seen on the monitors of Demarchy society, saw why it might make a difference to Abdhiamal. "Betha Torgussen was chosen to command the *Ranger* because she was the best qualified, and the best at making fast decisions. We all agreed to the choice." He tightened the jaws of a table clamp, not sure whether he was amused or annoyed. "Answer a personal question for me: What exactly do you think of my wife?" He watched an instinctive reaction rise up and die away before it reached Abdhiamal's lips. *An honest man . . .*

"I don't know." Abdhiamal frowned slightly, at nothing, at himself. "But I have to admit, she's made better decisions since I've known her than I have." He laughed once, looking away. "But then she chose space, instead of . . ." His eyes came back to Clewell; the frown and confusion filled them again.

"Why doesn't the Demarchy have women in space? My impression of Belter life was always that everyone did as they damn well pleased. Men and women."

"Before the war, maybe. But now we have to protect our women."

"From what? Living?" Clewell picked up the piece of wood, shifted it from hand to hand, annoyance overriding amusement now.

"From radiation!" It was the first time he had heard Abdhiamal raise his voice. "From genetic damage. The fission units that power our ships and factories are just too dirty. In spite of everythin' we've done, the number of defective births is twenty times as high as it was before the war."

Clewell thought of Bird Alyn. "What about men?"

"We can preserve sperm. Not ova."

"You've lost more than you know because of that war." Abdhiamal stood silently, expressionless. Clewell unstrapped the leather wristband that had been a parting gift from one of his sons, and held it out. "Do you recognize that symbol?" He pointed at the design enameled on a circle of copper, as Abdhiamal took it from his hand.

"*Yin* and *yang*?"

He nodded. "Do you know what it stands for?"

"No."

"It stands for Man and Woman. On Morningside, that means two equal halves merging into a perfect biological whole. A spot of white in the black, a spot of black in the white . . . to remind us that the genes of a man go into the creation of every woman, and the genes of a woman go into the creation of every man. We're not men and cattle, Abdhiamal, we're men and women. Our genes match; we're all human beings. It makes a lot of sense, when you stop to think about it."

"Odd–" Abdhiamal smiled again, noncommittal. "Somehow I didn't think *yin* and *yang* would have been a part of Morningside's cultural heritage."

"Your people and ours, all came from the same Old World in the beginning. In the beginning *yin* and *yang* didn't mean much to us. We had a lot of symbols to separate us, then. We just need one now."

"*Yin* and *yang* and the Viking Queen . . ." Abdhiamal murmured; his smile turned rueful. "And Wadie in Wonderland. Why were there more men than women in your—family?"

Because it happened to work out that way. Clewell almost answered him with the truth. He paused. "Son, if you have to ask me why a marriage needs more men than women, you're younger than I thought you were." He grinned. "And it's not because I'm slowing down."

Abdhiamal drew back, disbelief ruffling his decorum. He held out the wristband.

Clewell shook his head. "Keep it. Wear it. . . . Think about it, when you wonder why we're strangers to you."

Betha reentered the control room; Shadow Jack and Rusty still lay head-to-head on the grass-green rug. She moved quietly past them, sat down at the control board, and pulled Discus into focus on the screen, a small silver crescent like a thumbnail moon. All that mattered now, and nothing else. She would get this ship home; this time they *would* succeed. Nothing must get in the way of her purpose, no man, living or dead, no memory. . . .

Her torn hand burned. She pressed it down on the cold panel, leaving a spot of blood. Her mind crossed three light-years and half a lifetime to a factory yard on the Hotspot perimeter, where she had burned her hand on hot metal, inspecting the ideal made real. She had gone outside to see her first engineering design passing in sequence on the assembly line—unbearably silver in the blinding noon light, unbearably beautiful.

She was in the third quarter of her twentieth year, fresh from the icy terminator. The golden rain of heat, the battering flow of parched desert air on this, the perimeter of total desolation, dazed her; pride filled her with exhilaration, and there was a certain student-worker. . . . She waited for him to stand beside her and tell her that her design was beautiful. And then he would ask her– Rough gloves caught her arms and turned her back, "Hey, snowbird, you want to go blind?" She saw Eric van Helsing's adored, sunburned face laugh at her through the shield of his helmet, as she caught the padding of his insulated jacket. "They always said engineers were too quirky to come in out of the sun. You'd better go back."

"For a social scientist, you haven't learned much about motivation, Eric van Helsing." Angry because he had ruined everything–and because, like a fool, she had waited for him–she pulled away, almost ran back across the endless gravel yard, escaping into the cool, dazzled darkness inside the nearest building. She stood still in the corridor, fighting tears, and heard him come through the doors behind her. . . .

> You are the rain, my love, sweet water
> Flowing in the desert of my life. . . .

Someone entered the room; Betha smelled the scent of apples. She looked for Claire's smooth moon-round face and golden tangled curls . . . found Bird Alyn again, thin and brown and branch-awkward: a dryad in a pink pullover shirt and blue jeans, with flowers in her hair. . . . Bird Alyn, not Claire, who tended hydroponics now.

Shadow Jack stirred as Bird Alyn dropped down beside him, her freckled cheeks blushing dusky-rose. Betha turned back to the screen, hiding her smile.

". . . like some apples?"

"Oh . . . thanks, Bird Alyn." He laughed, self-conscious. "You always think of me."

She murmured something, questioning.

"What's the matter with you? No! How many times do I have to tell you that? Get out of here, leave me alone."

Pain knotted in Betha's stomach; she heard Bird Alyn climb to her feet and flee, stumbling on the doorsill. Betha turned in her seat to look at Shadow Jack; kneeling, he glared back at her as he pushed himself up.

"Maybe it's none of my business, Shadow Jack, but just what in hell is the matter with you?"

"There's nothin' the matter with me! You think everybody has to be like you? Everybody isn't; you're a bunch of dirty perverts!" His voice shook. "It makes me sick." He went out of the room. She heard him go down the steps too fast.

Betha sat very still, clutching the chair arms, wondering where she would find the strength to rise. . . . Rusty sidled against her legs, *mrr*ing. Stiffly she reached down, drew the cat up into her lap; hanging on to meaning, to the promise of a time when Heaven would be no more than one of countless stars lost behind the twilight. "Rusty, you're all the things I count on. What would I have done without you?" Rusty's rough, tiny tongue kissed the palm of her hand twice in gentle affection. "Oh, Rusty," she whispered, "you make misers of us all." Betha got to her feet slowly and looked toward the empty doorway.

Shadows moved silently over the tiles, moist and green, like the waters of a dream sea. Bird Alyn sobbed against the cold hexagonal tiles of the seat-back, touched by the fragile fingers of a hanging fern.

" . . . not fair, it's not fair . . ." Her love was an endless torment because it fed on dreams. He would never touch her, never stroke her hair . . . never love her, and she would never stop wanting his love.

She heard him enter the lab, and the sob caught in her throat. She pushed herself up, eyes shut, wetness dripping off her chin.

"Don't cry, Bird Alyn. It wastes water." Shadow Jack stood before her, hands at his sides, watching her tears drip down.

She opened her eyes, saw him through lashes starred with teardrops, felt more tears rise defiantly. "We have . . . plenty of water, Shadow Jack." Misery coiled inside her, tightening like a drawn spring. "We're not on Lansing; everything's different here!"

His eyes denied it; he said nothing, frowning.

She turned away on the bench. "But I'm not . . . I know I'm not. Why did this happen to me? Why am I so ugly, when I love you?"

He dropped down beside her on the seat, pulled her hands, one crippled and one perfect, down from her face. "Bird Alyn, you're not! You're not . . . you're beautiful." She saw her iamge in his eyes and saw that it was true. "But–you can't love me."

"I can't help it . . . how can I help it?" She reached out, her wet fingers brushed his face. "I love you."

He caught her roughly, arms closing over her back, and pulled her against him. She struggled in surprise, but his mouth stopped her cry, and then her struggling. ". . . love you, Bird Alyn . . . since forever . . . don't you know?"

Her outflung hands rose to tighten on his shoulders, drawing him into her dreams, joy filled her like song–

> Let me blossom first for you,
> Let me quench my thirst in you. . . .

"No—" He pulled back suddenly, letting her go. He leaned against the cold tiles, gulping air. "No. No. We can't." His hands made fists.

"But . . . you love me. . . ." Bird Alyn reached out, astonished by disappointment. "Why can't we? Please, Shadow Jack . . . please. I'm not afraid—"

"What do you want me to do, get you pregnant!"

She flinched, shaking her head. "It doesn't have to happen."

"It does; you know that." He sagged forward. "Do you want to feel the baby growin' in you and see it born . . . with no hands and no arms, or no legs, or no— To have to put it Out, like my mother did? We're defective! And I'll never let it happen to you because of me."

"But it won't. Shadow Jack, everything's different here on the ship. They have a pill, they never have to get pregnant. They'd let us . . ." She moved close, stroked the midnight blackness of his hair. "Even one pill lasts for a long time."

"And what about when they're gone?"

"We . . . we'd always have . . . memories. We'd know, we could remember how it felt, to touch, and kiss, and h-hold each other. . . ."

"How could I keep from touchin' you again, and kissin' you, and holdin' you, if I knew?" His eyes closed over desperation. "I couldn't. If I was never going to see you again . . . but I will. I'd see you every day for the rest of my life, and how could I stop it, then? How could you? It would happen."

She shook her head, pleading, her face burning, hot hopeless tears burning her eyes.

"I can't let go, Bird Alyn. Not now. Not ever. I couldn't stand what it would do to me . . . what it would do to you. Why did we ever see this ship! Why did this happen to us? It was all right till—until—" His hands caught together; he cracked his knuckles.

Softly she put out her own hand, catching his; fingers twined brown into bronze. Because of this ship their world would live . . . and because of it, nothing would ever be right in their lives again. She heard water dripping, somewhere, like tears; a dead blossom fell between them, clicked on the sterile tiles.

Betha left the doorway quietly, as she had come, and silently climbed the stairs.

RANGER (DISCAN SPACE) + 2.70 MEGASECONDS

Discus, a banded carnelian the size of a fist, set in a silver plane: The rings, almost edge-on, were a film of molten light streaked with lines of jet, spreading toward them on the screen. Wadie drifted in the center of the control room, keeping his thoughts focused on the silhouette that broke the foreground of splendor: Snows-of-Salvation, orbiting thirty Discus radii out, beyond the steep gradient depths of the gravity well. Snows-of-Salvation, that had been Bangkok on the prewar navigation charts, the major distillery for the Rings. It was one of five, but it outproduced the rest by better than ten to one; in part because its operations were powered by a nuclear battery constructed in the Demarchy, in part because it could send out shipments using a linear accelerator, also from the Demarchy but infinitely more useful here where transport distances were short. The Ringers' own primitive oxyhydrogen rockets made hopelessly inefficient tankers.

He remembered Snows-of-Salvation as it had been when he arrived with the Demarchy engineers: endless grayness honeycombing the ice and stone; a chill that crept into a man's bones until he couldn't remember warmth; a small gray population, a people renting space in purgatory. A people fanatical to the point of insanity, in the eyes of the Demarchy. He had been sent to keep demarch and Ringer from each others' throats—sent because no one better qualified had been willing to go. He had stayed to see that two incompatible and suspicious groups never forgot their common goal of increasing the supply of volatiles. And in the fifty megaseconds he had spent in his grim and lonely exile, he had come to know a number of men he could only call friends and had seen more of the Ringers' Grand Harmony than any other demarch. He had come to understand the chronically marginal life that existed for the Ringers everywhere; to see, almost painfully, what made them endure their oppressive collectivist ideology: the knowledge that they must always pull together or they would not survive....

The captain's voice drew him back. His eyes fixed on her where she hung before the viewscreen, her hair floating softly, free from gravity, her shirtsleeves rolled up to the elbow. He stared, the present an overlay on the past. The clean, colored warmth of the control room drove out a dreary poverty that made Morningside's plainness suddenly seem frivolous.

Morningside . . . could he ever have come to see its people as clearly as he had seen the Ringers? How long did it take to feel at ease with a people who offended your sense of propriety in every way imaginable? Whose behavior slipped through your attempts to categorize it the way water slipped between your fingers. . . . Four kilosecs ago he had come to the upper level to get himself some food and had found the captain and Welkin already in the dining hall and Bird Alyn playing her guitar. They had all been singing; as though in four thousand seconds they were not going to commit an act of piracy or face one more trial whose outcome meant freedom and life for all of them....

Together we find courage,
Our song will never cease....

Or perhaps, he had realized suddenly, they sang because they were much too aware and afraid of that fact. *Not what you sing, or how,* Welkin had said, *but how it makes you feel.* Suddenly aware of his own part in that coming trial, he had been drawn across the room to join them by something stronger than curiosity . . . only to have Betha Torgussen's face close and lose its warmth as she saw him; only to have her rise from the table, breaking the pattern of song, and abruptly leave the room.

". . . I can't believe this reading, Pappy. They should be frying down there, but they're not. There's no magnetosphere, no trapped radiation field. . . . Do you know anything about this, Abdhiamal?" The captain glanced over her shoulder at him, not quite meeting his eyes.

He looked past her at the screen. "This is Heaven, after all, Captain. Discus's radiation fields are strong enough, but they don't reach much higher than the rings. That was one of the things that brought us to this system—the rocks and snowballs around Discus are accessible as they never were around Old Jupiter." He caught her eyes. "You don't seem very concerned about whether *we* were fryin'?"

"We make good shielding on Morningside, or we'd have fried long ago." She broke away, as she always did, now; looked up at Bird Alyn hanging near the ceiling above her head. "Bird Alyn, find the local talk frequency for me." Her voice was calm.

Bird Alyn nodded, braced against the ceiling, and swooped down to the panel to catch up an earjack.

"Where's Shadow Jack?" Welkin asked.

Bird Alyn stared at the panel, said something inaudibly.

"What?"

". . . don't know . . . said . . . didn't think he could face . . ." She shrugged. The room filled with static as she switched on the receiver. The static slurred abruptly into words. The words sharpened as Bird Alyn locked them in. "Here . . ."

"What are they broadcasting?"

"They're talkin' to a ship, I think; a tanker. I heard 'hydrogen.' "

"Good—then let's rudely interrupt them." The captain reached for the broadcast button. "You're sure they'll know who we are, Abdhiamal?"

"I'm sure. Even the Ringers have had time to spread word of what happened to that ship by now. And if their propaganda is as extreme as it usually is, they'll expect you to be a butcher. They'll—respect your threat."

"All right." She wet her lips, pushed the button. "Snows-of-Salvation, Snows-of-Salvation, come in please . . ."

The speaker shrilled irritation; Bird Alyn jerked the earjack away from her head.

"Who is that? Get the hell off this freq! there's a mixed-load dockin' in progress here! Do you—"

The captain's hand on the button cut him off. "Tell them to hold off, we have something more important to say to you."

"Who is this?"

"This is . . ." She hesitated. ". . . the ship your Navy attacked two megaseconds ago . . . the ship from Outside." She released the button.

No answer came.

"You've impressed them." Wadie smiled, humorlessly.

A different voice came through, a voice that was strangely familiar to him, ordering the unseen tanker into a holding orbit. Welkin reached across the comm panel, by Bird Alyn's shoulder, and a new segment of the screen erupted into a blizzard of static snow. "We're receiving wideband." He typed a sequence on the console; abruptly the screen showed a squeezed triple image. He punched in a correction, and a single black-and-white picture re-formed. They saw a pinched face squinting from behind wire-rimmed spectacles: a middle-aged man in a heavy, quilted jacket and a thick knit cap. "We're transmitting compatible now, too," Welkin said. The captain nodded, seeming to take the old man's skill for granted.

"What is it you want here?" The familiar voice matched a familiar face, harsh with anger or fear. *With anger* . . . Djem Nakamore was too stubborn and dogmatic to acknowledge anything else. Wadie pushed out of his line of sight as Nakamore glared at Betha Torgussen.

Her face hardened, staring Nakamore down. "We want one thousand tons of processed hydrogen, sent out on the trajectory I give you to our ship. If you fail to do this, I'll destroy your distillery, and you'll all die." The hardness seemed to come easily; Wadie felt surprise.

He watched their expressions change, the two strangers in the background showing real fear. Nakamore stiffened upright, drifting off-center on the screen.

"You won't destroy us. Even the Demarchy would want you dead if you did that."

"We're not from your system; you're nothing to us. The Demarchy is nothing. I hope you all go to hell together for what you've done to us; but Snows-of-Salvation will get there first unless you obey my orders."

". . . they meant it . . ." a blurred voice said in the background. Nakamore turned away abruptly, cutting off sound. He spoke to the others, their eyes still flickering to the screen, faces tense, their breath frosting in the cold air as they spoke. Nakamore turned back to the panel, out of sight below him, and punched the sound on. "We don't have a thousand tons of hydrogen on hand. We never have that much, and we just sent out a big shipment."

Wadie shook his head. "They'd never let the supply get that low. The output is nearly three thousand tons per megasec, and they have at least four times that as backlog in case the distillery goes off-line for repairs."

The captain twisted to look at him, cutting off sound in return. "You're that familiar with their operation?"

He nodded. "I told you—I spent almost fifty million seconds down there. I saw that distillery put together and saw it go into operation. I know what it can do. And I know that man. . . ." He remembered Djem Nakamore's face, the bald head reddened by the light from a primitive methane-burning stove; remembered the amused face of Djem's visiting half-brother, Raul. He heard the hiss as water sweated from the ceiling to drop and steam on the stove's greasy surface, as he waited while Djem pondered his next painfully predictable move that would lose him his hundredth, or his thousandth, game of chess to Wadie Abdhiamal. Stubborn, didactic, and unimaginative . . . honest, forthright, and dedicated to his duty. No match, as Djem had told him, often enough and without resentment, for Wadie's own quick and devious mind—yet too stubborn not to go on trying to win. Wadie adjusted the earflaps of his heavy hat, put out a hand to move his queen, *Checkmate*. . . . "I know that man. Push him; he's not—devious enough to know whether you're bluffin'. And he'll do anything to keep that distillery intact." He realized suddenly that it could have been Raul instead who faced them now and was glad, for all their sakes, that it was not. He looked away as he spoke, avoiding the bright image on the screen and Betha Torgussen's eyes.

The captain frowned slightly, then turned back to

Nakamore on the screen. "I don't accept that. You have twenty-five thousand seconds to give us the hydrogen or be destroyed."

"That's impossible! . . . It would take at least a hundred thousand seconds."

"Lie," Wadie said softly, shook his head again. "He's stalling; Central Harmony keeps plenty of naval units in this volume, and he's hopin' some of 'em will get here in time."

Nodding, she repeated flatly, "You have twenty-five kiloseconds. I know you have a high-performance linear accelerator down there. Use it. I don't want any manned vehicles to approach us. Copy coordinates . . ." She spoke the numbers carefully.

As she finished speaking Nakamore looked past her, angry and beaten, but little of it showing on his face. "Are you there givin' her the answers, Wadie?"

Wadie hung motionless . . . speechless. He pushed away from the panel at last, out into Nakamore's view. "Yeah, Djem, it's me."

"We picked up the broadcast debates from the Demarchy—how they've outlawed you. I figured maybe you'd . . ." Nakamore's face set, with the righteous anger of a man to whom loyalty was everything; with the pain of a man betrayed by a friend. "We were fools not to see what you and your . . . starship aliens would try. Why stop with a thousand tons of hydrogen? Why not take it all?"

"One thousand tons of hydrogen is all we need, Djem. And we need it bad, or I wouldn't put you through this." Without fuel, the starship was trapped, prey to the first group quick enough to take it. And then the Grand Harmony, the Demarchy, and everyone else would be the prey. Then the threats would be no bluff. This was for the best; this was the only choice he could possible make, the only sane choice.

If he could only . . . He started, "Djem, I—" But no words would come.

Nakamore waited, his black eyes pitiless. At last he leaned forward, reaching for the unseen panel. "Traitor." His face disappeared; and with it the last chance of asylum for a banished man. Discus alone lay on the screen.

The captain sat gazing fixedly at the screen, her mouth pressed together, a brittle golden figurine. Welkin glanced at Wadie, apologetic but saying nothing, saving him from the embarrassment of a witty response that wouldn't come.

". . . think they'll do it?" Bird Alyn pulled at the flapping end of her belt. "What if they don't?"

"They will." He found his voice, and his composure. "In fifty million seconds, Djem Nakamore never won a game of chess from me."

"You were perfect, Betha." Welkin turned back, his faded eyes searching the captain's downturned face. "Eric couldn't have put it more convincingly."

"If Eric were alive, we wouldn't be doing this."

Wadie nodded, relieved. "I almost believed you meant every word of that, myself."

She struck a match. "What makes you think I didn't, Abdhiamal?" She lit her pipe, facing him with the same hardness that had faced down Snows-of-Salvation. "What have the Ringers done for us lately?"

"Indeed." He bowed grimly, looked back at Welkin. "I've learned my lesson—I'll never insult another engineer." He pushed off toward the door.

Betha watched him disappear down the stairwell, shaken with the coldness that left her words of apology stillborn.

"Betha . . . would you . . . are you really goin' to

. . . destroy the distillery?" Bird Alyn whispered unhappily.

Bertha met the frightened face. "No, of course not, Bird Alyn I wouldn't do that. I'm not really a–a butcher."

Bird Alyn nodded, blinking, maneuvered backward and started for the door.

Clewell rubbed his beard. "Then why act like one, Betha? That was a little too convincing for me, too. Or isn't it an act any more?"

Shame warmed her face, drove the coldness from her. "You know it is, Pappy! But that damned Abdhi-amal–"

Clewell lifted his head slightly, unfastened his seat-belt. "He's not such a bad sort . . . for a 'damned fop.' He's held up pretty well under one gee . . . under everything he's been through." Meaning that she hadn't made things any easier.

"He's a phony; he's lucky he didn't cripple himself." She looked away irritably.

"He's a proud man, Betha. He might not call it that . . . but anybody who can stand straight and smile while gravity's pulling him apart–or loyalty is–has my admiration. In a way, he reminds me of–"

"He's not at all like Eric."

His eyebrows rose. "That wasn't what I was going to say. He reminds me of you." He held up a hand, cutting off her indignation. "But now that you mention it, there is something about him . . . a manner, maybe; even a physical resemblance. Maybe it's why I like him in spite of myself; maybe it's what bothers you. Something does."

"Oh, Pappy . . ." She lifted her hand, pressing her rings against her mouth. "It is true. Every time I look at him, anything he does, he reminds me–But he's *not* Eric. He's not one of us, he's one of *them*. How can I feel this way? How can I stop wanting . . .

wanting . . ." She reached out; Clewell's firm, weathered hand closed over her wrist.

He smoothed her drifting hair. "I don't know. I don't know the answer, Betha." He sighed. "I don't know why they claim age is wisdom. Age is just getting old."

Shadow Jack moved restlessly, trapped in the too-empty box of the room where he slept, haunted by the ghost of a stranger: manuals on economics, a nonsense song lyric, a hand-knit sweater suspended in midair—a dead man's presence scattered through drawers and cupboards in the clutter of a life's detritus. Rusty clung to his shoulders, her mute acceptance easing the shame of his exile. He stroked her mindlessly, hearing only the ticking of the clock; meaningless divisions marking the endless seconds. He wondered whether they would get what they wanted from the Ringers, wondered how he could face Betha Torgussen again . . . wondered how he would face the rest of his life.

Rusty's small, inhuman face rose from his shoulder, her ears flicking. "Bird Alyn?" He pushed to the doorway, saw Wadie Abdhiamal disappear into another room. He heard Abdhiamal's voice, almost inaudible: "Damn that woman! She'd spit in the eye of God."

Shadow Jack moved along the hall, stopped at Abdhiamal's doorway, staring, "What's the matter, she spit in your eye?"

Abdhiamal twisted, a split-second's exasperation on his face. He smoothed his work shirt absently, smoother his expression. "Yeah . . . somethin' like that."

"What happened up there? Did we get the hydrogen?"

"Probably. . . . Why weren't you in the control room?"

He grimaced. "I couldn't do it. I—I called the captain a pervert."

"You what?" Abdhiamal frowned in disbelief.

Shadow Jack caught the doorway to move on, desperation turned him back. "Can . . . I talk to you . . . man to man?"

Abdhiamal gestured him into the room, no trace of amusement on his face. "Probably. What about?"

Shadow Jack cleared his throat; Rusty pushed off from his shoulder, rose like a lifting ship, and swam toward Abdhiamal. "How come you never married?"

Abdhiamal laughed, startled. "I don't know." He watched the cat, reached out to pull her down to his chest. "Maybe because I never met a woman who'd spit in the eye of God."

Shadow Jack's eyes widened; and looking at Abdhiamal, he wondered who was more surprised.

Abdhiamal laughed again, shrugged. "But somehow I doubt it."

"I mean . . . you said before, that now you never would get married. I thought there was—some other reason." He reached for the doorframe.

"There was."

He stopped, holding on.

"I've traveled a lot. That means I've been exposed to high radiation levels and potential genetic damage. We have ways of preservin' sperm so men at least can travel and still raise healthy children. But with the bill of attainder, I'm legally dead now. They'll destroy my account." Abdhiamal took a deep breath. "And I've been sterilized."

Shadow Jack looked back, letting the words come. "I'd be happy if I was sterile!" He shook his head. "I didn't mean . . . I didn't mean it like that. But we can't ever get married, Bird Alyn and me, because I'm not sterile and she's not. We *are* defective. We shouldn't ever have children, but we would. . . ."

Abdhiamal scratched Rusty under the chin. "It's a simple operation. Can't they perform it on Lansing?"

"They could . . . but they won't." Misery hung on him like a weight. "If you're a Materialist, you're supposed to take responsibility for your own actions. You're supposed to take the consequences, not expect anybody else to do it for you. Like my mother, when my sister was born an' they said she was too defective . . . my mother had to put her Out. . . . She wouldn't let my father touch her any more." He looked down at his hands. "But the medical technology's bad anyhow. Sometimes I think they just don't want to waste what's left."

Abdhiamal's voice was gently professional. "How were you judged defective? You look sound to me."

Shadow Jack's hands tightened on metal. "Maybe I wasn't defective, then. But my sister was. And they needed more outside workers, so they told me I had to work on the surface. That's what you do if you're marginally damaged, like Bird Alyn. That's where I met her. . . ." Where he had discovered what life must have been like once, lived in the beauty of gardens and not the bleakness of stone. And where he had discovered that his own life did not end because he had left the shielding walls of rock; that feeling did not, or belief, or hope. But he had spent too many megaseconds mending a tattered world-shroud, too many megaseconds in a contaminated ship. . . . And there were no miracles to heal a crippled hand or mend a broken heart.

He struck the doorframe. "Everything goes wrong! I didn't mean to call Betha . . . what I called her. But she had so many husbands; she even has children!

When Bird Alyn and I can't even have each other . . . it just made me crazy. Betha lost so much, and I said–I said that to her. She helped us after we tried to take her ship just like everybody else–"

"You did? And she let you get away with it?"

He nodded, feeling ridiculous. "All we had was a can opener . . . I guess she thought we were fools."

"And–you said she has children?" Abdhiamal looked down at the wide leather band circling his wrist.

"Yeah. Goin' into space is like . . . like doing anything else to them. It's not the end of anything." He bit his tongue, remembering that it had been for the crew of the *Ranger*.

"If she forgave you for trying to steal her ship, I expect she'll forgive you for callin' her a pervert. Sooner than she'll forgive me for makin' remarks about engineers."

Shadow Jack frowned, not understanding.

Abdhiamal's smile faded. "It seems you and I have more than one problem in common. Like every group in Heaven Belt shares the problems of every other one. And I'm not so sure any more that there's an easy answer for any of us."

Shadow Jack turned away, saw Bird Alyn watching him from the end of the hall. He met her eyes, hopelessness dragging him down like the chains of gravity. "There aren't any answers at all. I should have known that. Sorry to take up your time, Abdhiamal."

Wadie closed the door, still cradling the cat absently against his side. In his mind he saw the future on Lansing, grief and death among the gardens–and saw in Lansing the future of all Heaven. . . . *The fu-*

ture? Silence pressed his ears, deafening him. *The end.* The Demarchy was only one more fading patch of snow. There was no answer. Nothing he could ever do—nothing he had ever done—would hold back Death. He had made himself believe that his work had some relevance and worth, that a kind of creation existed in his negotiations, a binding force to keep equilibrium with disintegration and decay. But he had been wrong. It had always been too late. He was a damned fop, living at the expense of everyone else . . . and wasting his life on the self-delusion that he was somehow saving them all. Wasting his life: he had thrown away his last chance of ever having a life of his own, a home, a family, any real relationship. And all that he had ever done, been, or believed was meaningless. It had all been for nothing—and it would all be nothing in the end. *Nothing.*

Rusty squirmed in his grasp like an impatient child. As he released her his arm scraped the ventilator screen, his hand closed over a flat, palm-sized square trapped by the soft exit of air. He pulled it down, stared at it. A picture—a hologram—of a man and a woman, each holding a child, flooded in blazing light where they stood before an ugly, half-sunken dwelling. The woman was Betha Torgussen, her hair long, coiled on her head in braids. And the man, tall, with dark hair and a lean, sunburned face . . . *Eric?* Her voice came to him suddenly, from behind a shielding faceplate, in a train car on Mecca. *I—I thought you were someone I knew.* Wadie brushed the images with a finger, moving through them. Ghosts . . .

Betha Torgussen's voice came to him out of a speaker on the wall, telling the crew that Nakamore had acquiesced.

RANGER (DISCAN SPACE) + 2.74 MEGASECONDS

"Okay, Pappy, the cables are secured. We really outdid ourselves when we closed with this load! Start us in." Betha raised her chin from the speaker button, hooking her arm under the twisted strength of the steel cable, secure in the crevice between cylinders of hydrogen. She felt the abrupt lurch as the winches started the final shipment of fuel moving in toward the looming brilliance of the *Ranger*.

"This is the lot, Betha." Clewell's voice filled her helmet, smiling. She imagined his smile, felt it through the ship's mirrored hull.

"This is it. We've done it, Pappy! We're really going to make it." Through the shielded faceplate of her helmet she saw the molten silver, the ruby scarab of Discus reflecting on the *Ranger*'s hull, rising above a dull-green horizon of clustered tanks, marred by a tiny spot of blackness. The shadow of Snows-of-Salvation . . . or a ragged hole torn in the metal. She looked away, dizzy, past the small bright-suited figure of Shadow Jack at one end of the fifty-meter-long bundled cylinders. And out into the void; imagined the merciless drag of the Discan gravity well pulling her loose into the endless night . . . like five others before her. She shut her eyes, clung to the cable; opened them again to look down at the solid surface of the tanks, along the dull greenness at Abdhiamal, inept and uncommunicative at the shipment's other limit. They were almost flush now with the *Ranger's* massive protection; it would be over soon. *One more, just one more time. . . .* Sweat tickled her face; she shook her head angrily inside her helmet. *Damn it! You won't fall—*

"Betha!" It was Bird Alyn's voice, rising clearly for once above the crackle of her feeble helmet speaker. Betha saw her, gnatlike beside the immense holding rack clamped to the ship's skin. "The load's not closing even! . . . Abdhiamal, your end—the end cable's caught between tanks—"

"I'll clear it."

"Abdhiamal, wait!" Betha saw him go over the end, saw the flash of his guidance rocket as he disappeared. "Pappy! Loosen the aft cable, right now!" She pulled her own guidance unit loose from the catch at her waist, pressed the trigger, sent herself after him to the end of the world. Looking over, she saw him hovering near the hub of the wheel of tanks, the cable trapped between two cylinders. She saw him catch hold of the cable, brace his feet, and pull—"Abdhiamal, stop, stop!"—saw the cable slip free . . . watched as the bound tanks recoiled below her and the cable wrenched loose from the hull, arcing soundlessly toward her like a striking snake. She backed desperately, knowing, knowing—

"Clewell!" Her face cracked against the helmet glass in starbursts of light as the cable struck her across the chest, throwing her out and away from the ship. She fought for breath, blood in her mouth, her lungs crippled with pain, saw the ship like a fiery pinwheel slip out of her view, blackness, blood and molten silver, blackness. . . . She fumbled for the trigger of her guidance rocket, but her hands were empty. And she was falling.

No— Betha began to scream.

* * *

Wadie felt the cable slip loose as the captain's voice reached him, telling him to stop. He fell back, suddenly unsupported, looking up in surprise—to see what he had done, see the tanks rebound, the cable lash out like a whip and knock her away . . . saw her guidance rocket fly free, tumbling, a spark of light. "Oh, my God—" He heard the cried of Bird Alyn and Shadow Jack, echoing his own, no sound from Betha Torgussen; waved the others back as he went after her into the night.

The immensity of isolation stifled him, filling the black-and-brilliant desolation like sand, dragging at him, holding him back . . . as the isolation of his own making had cut him off from truth all his life. He closed with her spiraling form slowly, agonizingly, centimeters every second . . . seeing in his mind a ruptured suit, a frozen corpse, her pale, staring face cursing him even in death for the hypocrisy of his wasted years. Yet wanting, more than he had ever wanted anything in his life, to close that gap between them, and see instead that it was not too late. . . .

And after a space as long as his life his gloved hand clamped over an ankle. He drew her toward him and used his guidance unit to stop their outward fall. He caught her helmet in his hands, felt her clutch him feebly as he searched behind the silent, red-fogged glass for a glimpse of her face. Repeating, wild with relief, "Betha . . . Betha . . . Betha, are you all right?"

Her shadowed face fell forward, peering out; her chin pressed the speaker button. "Eric . . . oh, Eric." He heard her sob. "Don't let me go . . . I'll fall . . . don't let go, don't let go . . ." Her arms tightened convulsively, silence formed between them again. He stroked the tempered glass, "I won't . . . it's all right . . . I won't let you go." The plane of the Discan rings blinded him with frigid glory, as immutable as death; he turned away from it, started them back toward the diminished ship, across the black sand desert of the night. She kept radio silence; he did not search for her face again behind the blood-reddened glass, granting her the privacy of her grief, feeling the ghosts of five human beings move with them. And at last he heard her voice say his own name, thanking him, and say it again. . . .

"What happened?"

"Is she all right?"

"Betha, are you all right?"

The voices of Shadow Jack and Bird Alyn clamored in his helmet as they met him, their hidden faces turned toward Betha, gloved hands reaching out.

"She's hurt. Help me get her inside." She scarcely moved against his hold, silent as they made their way through the airlock.

They entered the control room, her hands still locked rigidly on his suit. He looked across the room at the panel, looking for Welkin; cleared his faceplate, suddenly aware that nothing moved. "Welkin?" He saw a hand, motionless above the chair arm, and his throat closed.

Betha raised her head as if she were listening, but he could not answer. She released her grip, pushing away from him. "Pappy?" Her voice quavered, she folded into a tight crescent in the air, her arms wrapped against her stomach. "Pappy . . . are you there?" He heard a small gasp as she tried to lift her hands. "Somebody . . . get this helmet off. I can't see. Pappy?"

"Betha—" Shadow Jack began, broke off.

Bird Alyn moved to release Betha's helmet, lifted it slowly, jerked back at the sight of her face filmed with blood.

But Betha had already turned away, shaking her

head to clear her confusion, pulling distractedly at her gloves. She froze as she saw the old man's drifting hand. "Oh, Jesus." Her own hand flew out, caught at Bird Alyn's suit, groping for purchase. Bird Alyn put an arm around her, helped her cross the room. Wadie followed.

"Pappy . . ." Her voice broke apart as she reached him.

Welkin opened his eyes as she touched his face, stared her into focus uncomprehendingly, his right hand pressing his chest. She laughed, or sobbed, squeezing his shoulder. "Thank God! Thank God . . . I thought . . . you're so cold . . ."

"Betha. Are you—?"

"I'm all right. I'm fine." She put a trembling hand up to her face, glanced at her bloody fingertips. "Just a . . . nosebleed. What—what happened?"

"Pain . . . in my chest, like being crushed; down my arm . . . must be my heart. Was afraid to move. When I saw . . . what happened to you on the screen—"

"Don't. Don't think about it . . . it's over. We'll make it, Pappy. We'll make it yet. Close your eyes, don't move, don't worry, just rest. We'll take care of you." She managed a smile, new blood blurring on her chin, her hand gently cupping his face.

"Should we get him to the infirmary?" Wadie hesitated near her shoulder, forcing himself to speak.

"No." Welkin shook his head, eyes shut. "Not yet. Finish the job!"

"He's right. We shouldn't move him yet, anyway. Thank God we're in zero gee. . . ." Betha pulled a scarf out of a cubby under the panel, starting a small blizzard of papers drifting. She wiped her face and spat gingerly, wincing. Wadie saw her control slip again, saw pain show, and her body bend as she pushed out of Welkin's sight. Bird Alyn moved back to her side, mouth open; she frowned, straightening, shook her head. "All right. Pappy said it. We're going to finish the job. Nothing will stop us now! I'll start the winch. Bird Alyn, get back outside . . . and make sure the load is secured. Shadow Jack, you'll chart us a course for Lansing. Tell me what you need to know, I'll double-check you. . . . Abdhiamal–"

He met her eyes, bracing against what he expected to see. "Keep the hell out of your way?"

Expressionless, she said, "Go to the infimary and get me a hypo of painkiller for Clewell. They're prefilled, with the first-aid supplies." She caught hold of a chair back, shook her head. "Make it two hypos. And then"–her eyes changed, clung to him–"keep the hell out of my way, Abdhiamal!"

GRUSINKA-MARU (IN TRANSIT, DEMARCHY TO DISCUS) + 2.75 MEGASECONDS

". . . how you intend to explain what your man's done now, MacWong? He must've shown the Outsiders how to get that hydrogen. Now he's made certain we can't catch the starship before it leaves the system." Esrom Tiriki moved incautiously in the overcrowded space of the ship's control room.

"He isn't 'my man' any more, Demarch Tiriki. He was declared a traitor," Lije MacWong repeated weaily. *He is a traitor, much to my surprise. Why? Revenge? A reasonable assumption. . . .*" "In any case, he didn't deliver the starship to the Ringers, either."

"But you said he would."

"It was a reasonable assumption." MacWong felt unaccustomed tension tightening the muscles in his neck—brought on by the discomfort of the ship's acceleration, and by the effect discomfort was having on everyone else, as well. He silently regretted the ill fortune that had made Tiriki Distillates a part owner of this fusion ship, and permitted Esrom Tiriki to be here as its representative. Tiriki—and his company—had suffered considerable embarrassment when their personal plans for the starship had been exposed; even Tiriki's two fellow representatives had begun to let their disapproval show as their tempers shortened. MacWong further regretted that Tiriki did not have the self-control to suffer in silence.

The Nchibe representative drew Tiriki's unwelcome attention again and MacWong drifted away past a yawning, fawning mediaman in Nchibe livery. They had picked up the Ringers' reply to the starship's threats, and it had been sent on to the Demarchy—as all crucial information was, and would be, during their pursuit. The people, the changeable god to whom he had offered up Wadie Abdhiamal and other sacrificial scapegoats, kept watch over him even here. But now for once the people kept their silence, because any response would have reached the starship too, and revealed their pursuit. For possibly the only time in his career he had a measure of freedom in his decision-making; he was not sure yet how much he could afford to enjoy it.

Because the next decision he would make now—and answer for later—was whether to continue pursuing the starship or to return to the Demarchy. And the decision was not as obvious as it seemed. . . . The starship had taken a thousand tons of hydrogen—far more than it needed to escape from the system, from what Osuna had told him. Enough fuel to critically cripple its speed and maneuverability. Had they done that for revenge, too? Somehow he doubted it. They had destroyed a ship before; this time they could have destroyed so much more . . . they could have destroyed the major distillery. But they hadn't. He experienced a curious mingling of fascination and relief.

But the starship had gone to Lansing when it first entered the system; there had been a Lansinger with the woman at Mecca. If its crew had made some sort of deal with Lansing, that could explain a lot of things. And it would mean that the starship would not be heading directly out of the system; that there was still a chance for Demarchy ships to overtake it.

MacWong looked back as the ship's pilot approached Tiriki and the others, to interrupt them deferentially. And what would happen if they captured the starship? He glanced out of the port beside him, seeing the long, intensely lavender thread of a second ship's torch reaching across the night. By then they would be millions of kilometers from the Demarchy—these three armed ships, and the men who controlled them: ambitious men, men who enjoyed power, men like Esrom Tiriki. No matter what the people decided concerning the starship, by then there would be no way that the Demarchy could force these men to obey it . . . and no one would be quicker to realize that. His nearness to Tiriki and his insulation from the people had made him understand what Abdhiamal had known instinctively from the start: that the starship which could be their salvation could instead turn out to be the bait for a deadly trap.

He sighed. *You were always a better man than I was, Wadie; and that was your whole problem. . . .* And maybe that explained Abdhiamal's treason better than any speculation about revenge. He had been more than sorry to make Abdhiamal into a man without a world . . . but maybe in the end it would turn out to be the best move he had ever made. And perhaps now he had the opportunity to repay Abdhiamal in part, as the spokesman of the people—by keeping his mouth shut about what he knew.

"Demarchs—" The three company men and the pilot looked up at him together; he watched a mediaman adjust a camera lens. "I think we all know by now that our attempt to seize the starship has failed. But at least it hasn't fallen into enemy hands. It's leavin's the system; we might as well save a further waste of our own resources and return home—"

"Maybe we haven't lost it yet, Demarch MacWong." Tiriki showed him a porcelain smile that was somehow more unpleasant than his former petulance.

"We've just been given some new information

about the starship." The Estevez nephew nodded at the ship's pilot. "Lin-piao says that the ship isn't leavin' the system; it's turned back in toward the Main Belt."

"To Lansing," Tiriki said. "They're goin' back to Lansing."

"We still have a chance to take it; Lin-piao says it's only doing one-quarter gee now."

MacWong hesitated, seeing the three of them united, finally, in the purpose of carrying through their mission. And behind them the entire Demarchy watched in silent judgment. It knew what they knew; and it knew that he, MacWong, had instigated this pursuit. The people didn't know everything—but had they already learned too much? He could still press for a retreat . . . but would they accept it now? "If the people feel that a further effort to pursue the starship wouldn't be worth the Demarchy's while, I hope they'll let us know." He spoke the words to the waiting cameras with careful emphasis. "In the meantime . . ." He felt the intentness of seven sets of eyes, felt the pressure of a thousand more behind them. "In view of this new information, I feel we should continue our mission. I have personal data, concernin' the starship's entry into the system and its fuel needs, that support the theory it's headin' for Lansing now." *Sorry, Wadie.* He watched the faces relax into satisfaction and complacency. *But it's my job to give the people what they want.* He matched them smile for smile, one satisfaction for another.

"Demarchs . . ." The pilot pulled self-consciously at the hem of his golden company jacket. "By the time we've changed course, we still may not be able to catch up with 'em. Even if the starship can only manage one-quarter gee, by the time we decelerate again for Lansing ourselves—"

The pilot broke off, as a frown spread among them

like a disease. MacWong weighed its significance like a physician; and prescribed the remedy that he knew would heal any damage to his own credibility: "I think that may not turn out to be a problem, demarchs. If you'll consider the followin' course of action. . . ."

RANGER (IN TRANSIT DISCUS TO LANSING) + 2.96 MEGASECONDS

Wadie walked the corridor to Betha Torgussen's private room, slowed by one-quarter gravity and the fatigue of their work in space . . . and by the same tangle of emotion that drove him to face her now. The memory of the Discan sky, hazed with shining flotsam and hung with crescent moons, haunted him: the knowledge of a costly victory won and almost lost again by his own actions; two lives, the last of the Morningside crew, almost lost—and with them the part of himself that he had only just begun to discover. . . .

He reached the open door, stopped as the hallway slipped back into focus, and stepped through.

Rusty's head appeared suddenly from a cocoon of bedding, watched him like a familiar as he looked across the room. The captain sat at her desk, her back to him, her attention lost among scattered displays and printouts. Empty coffee cups littered the desk top; there was a sign above her head on the wall, TEN YEARS AGO I COULDN'T EVEN SPELL "ENGINEER," AND NOW I ARE ONE. He smiled briefly, until he heard her sigh, a sound that was a small groan. The vision formed inside his eyes of her cracked and bandaged ribs, a bruise the width of his arm.

He turned abruptly to leave the room again, found a picture on the wall inside a broad green arrow pointing DOWN: found Betha Torgussen, and Welkin, and—Eric, bearded now and smiling. With them, two more women, two more men, and seven children bundled in heavy clothes; all pale, laughing, waving in three dimensions, joyfully disheveled against a background of snow. A family who knew how to share . . . and somehow, with the fever of futile greed that burned through Heaven, their sharing no longer seemed to alien or so bizarre. . . .

Rusty stirred on the bed, blinking; she *mrr*ed inquiringly. Betha turned across the back of her chair, controlling a grimace, her own eyes suddenly quick and nervous, questioning his presence.

"Betha . . . I'd like to see you, if you don't mind. There're some things I think I need to say." He crossed the room.

"All right, Abdhiamal." Her eyes went to his wrist, Clewell's wristband. "Yes, maybe you should." Her face changed. "But first, tell me how Clewell is. How is he taking the acceleration?"

"Well enough, I guess. He's very weak, but he's no fool. . . ." *And nobody's fool.* Sudden appreciation for the old man filled him. "I don't suppose I'd have the guts to be here if I didn't believe he was goin' to be all right. . . . But what about you? What are you tryin' to prove? Why the hell aren't you getting some rest—" He broke off, not sure who he was really angry at.

Her bruised mouth tightened. "Because I'd rather be sore than dead. And yes, I am trying to prove something." She gestured at the computer terminal, her expression easing. "I—didn't know whether to let you know about this, but . . . we've detected a patch of hydrogen and helium, Doppler-shifted into the red; I think it's a hydrogen fusion torch pointed away from us. Right now it's still thirty million kilometers behind us—but we're being followed."

"You can detect an averted torch at that range?

Your instruments are better than ours." He was impressed again.

"Are they? Good. . . . But with these fuel canisters strapped to the hull, we can't move faster than whoever's behind us. What I need to know is whether the ships come from the Demarchy or Discus; and, if they are from the Demarchy, what you think their mission is. Do they still want to take the ship, or are they out to destroy us?"

He leaned on the desk, the tendons ridging slightly in his arm. "Good question. The ships are from the Demarchy. Nobody else has anythin' like that left; the Ringers have only oxyhydrogen rockets. Our—the Demarchy's—fusion ships are owned by interests in the most powerful tradin' companies, but in times of 'national emergency' the Demarchy commandeers 'em. Which means MacWong's story about my handing you to the Ringers must've been well received. . . ." He stopped. "He knows it was a damn lie; and knowin' him, I'd say that means he did it because he still wants this ship, and that was the only way he could think of to get the ships to follow you."

"But then he must know that we'll still outrun them, now that we've got the fuel; even if we stop at Lansing. If they have to do a turnaround to match our deceleration we'll be long gone before they reach us. If they don't slow down, they'll overshoot . . . and all they could do then would be destroy us in passing." Her fingers tapped nervously.

He nodded. "He'd know that too. But he wants that ship intact for the Demarchy, and he's not the kind to mine quartz and think it's ice. He's got somethin' planned but I don't know what."

"At least we know where they are, and they don't know we know. If they were counting on surprise to close the gap they've lost it." She shifted in her seat, leaning hard on the desk top. "I suppose we'll know more when we begin decelerating and see if they do the same. Even if they don't slow down . . . well, depending on what you can tell me about the range of their weapons, I think we can still stop at Lansing long enough to off load the extra hydrogen—and then accelerate at right angles to them with enough time to get away. By the time they can change course, we'll be out of this system forever."

"Out of our system forever. And we'll be . . ." He looked down at her strong and gentle face, wondered why he had ever thought it was plain. His hands tightened over a sudden desire to touch it.

Realization colored her cheeks. She looked up at him strangely, almost welcoming, lifted a hand. "Sit down, Abdhiamal . . . Wadie Abdhiamal. You'll be—better off without us, yes."

He sank down on the padded wall seat, pushing aside heaped clothes. "Betha, there're no words to apologize for what we've done to you. And when it comes to things I've done to you, out of my own stupidity . . . my God, I nearly—killed you. All the things I said, not meanin'—"

Her hand waved the words to silence. "I never meant to ruin your life, Wadie. . . . I owe you as many apologies as you owe me. More. Is it too late to cancel them all out, now?"

He leaned back, resting his head against the wall, eyes on her. "It's never too late. But I'm not—very good at expressing my emotions, Betha. I'm not even good at admitting them to myself." He took a long breath. "All of a sudden there are a lot of things I want to be different. But there's so little time—" He broke off; feeling the presence of ghosts. "That picture across the room: Is that—Eric, beside you?"

Surprise caught her. She nodded, her face composed. "He was my first husband. He was—a kind of negotiator too, an ombudsman. We were monogamous for eight years before we married into Clewell's family."

"And you have children?"

"The twins, Richard and Kirsten; the boy and girl in front of me. They're about eleven now. . . ." She smiled. "They're all my children. But the twins were born to me, they have my name. All seven of our kids who are still at home are staying with my family."

"You left your children—" He stopped himself before he hurt her again. *We do change; but change always comes too fast . . . and too late.* And there were only one hundred kiloseconds remaining until they reached Lansing.

She glanced at him, puzzled. "Yes. We left them with my parents, on their tree farm." And understanding, "Half the world is your family when you're growing up on Morningside. They hug you, tell you stories, and make you toys . . . there's always someone who's glad to see you. We didn't abandon our children. But it has been very hard to miss seeing so much of their lives as they grow. At least Clewell and I will still get to see how they've grown. . . ." She looked down, shuffling papers; he saw the return of more than one kind of pain.

"Shadow Jack and Bird Alyn . . . are they why you're risking everything, to buy a dyin' world a few more seconds?"

She hesitated. "I don't know. I hadn't thought . . . but I suppose maybe it is. I wish—I wish I knew how to do more."

"You know, then? What it's like for them on Lansing?"

She nodded.

"I'm not much lookin' forward to it myself, I've got to admit. But I've talked myself out of anythin' better—literally." He smiled. "I don't regret it. It was in a good cause."

She picked up a cup, set it down aimlessly. "What will you do, Wadie, on Lansing?"

He smiled again, hearing his name; the smile stopped when he remembered. "Sit and watch the world end, I suppose. All the worlds. Not with a bang but a gasp."

"You don't have to, you know."

He felt her touch him as though she had raised a hand. He shook his head. "Maybe I do. Maybe that's my penance for pretendin' there was no tomorrow."

"You don't believe that?"

"I don't know." He shrugged. "I don't know what I believe any more." Only knowing that he was alive in a vast mausoleum and afraid to look at death. "But I belong here, to Heaven; if that makes any sense. It scares the hell out of me, but I've got to see it through. But thanks." He saw her smile, disappointed.

"You can change your mind."

"Sooner than I could change Heaven. . . . Ironic, isn't it; that we began with everything and Morningside with nothing . . . and look who failed."

"We almost failed too—more than once." Betha stared at the wall, looking through time. "So did Uhuru, and Hellhole, and Lebensraum. But we had help."

"From where?"

"From each other. Planets like Morningside are so marginal any small setback becomes a disaster . . . but they're the most common kind of habitable world; they're all like Morningside in our volume of space. But our worlds are within reach of one another. We set up a trade ring, and when one of us falls flat, the rest pick it up and put it back together. And that's how we survive. That's all we do; we survive. But it's enough . . . it'll have to be enough forever, now that our journey here has failed.

"We have our own ironies, you know. . . . Morningside was settled after a major political upheaval on Earth. Our nearest neighbor now, Uhuru, was settled by some of our former 'enemies' after their own empire on Old Earth fell. Need makes stranger bedfellows than politics ever did."

He laughed abruptly. "As the five of us should know."

"Yes." She held him with her eyes, fingers over her lips.

"If you'd come before the war, Betha, maybe the five of us would even be doin' some good. Heaven could have learned somethin' then about sharing. Now it's too late; there's nothing left to share."

She shifted position again, wincing. "Wadie . . . you said the knowledge that put Heaven's technology where it was is still intact. That if you could rebuild your capital industry, you could still make the Belt work again, and it could be everything it once was. You said even the *Ranger* could make the difference. . . . What if—what if we tied you into our trading network? It's feasible; the distance here from Morningside isn't that much greater than the distances we already travel. If we gave you the means for recovery, you could give us what we wanted all along, a richer life for all our worlds—and you'd never have to see this happen again!"

He listened to her voice come alive with inspiration; felt suddenly as though the pain and grief had lifted from her mind only to settle in his own. "That's what I said. But I was wrong."

"Wrong?"

"We've gone down too far. We can't recover now; death is a disease that's infected us all. We'll never work together now, even to save ourselves."

"But if they could understand that there was hope for all of them . . ."

"How would you make them understand? You've

seen how well they listen." He slammed his hand down on the bench. "They wouldn't listen!"

"No, they wouldn't. . . ." Betha began to smile, in misery, moving her head from side to side. "Wadie Abdhiamal–how did we come to this? You saying they wouldn't, me saying they would. . . . How could we come to understand each other better than we understand ourselves?"

He shook his head, felt a smile soothe his own mouth, lost his useless anger watching her.

Her hand moved tentatively from the desk to touch the leather band on his wrist; he caught her hand and their fingers twined, brown and pale. She looked across at him, down at their hands. She drew her hand from his again, said quietly to no one, "And not one of them lived happily ever after. . . ."

FLAGSHIP UNITY (LANSING SPACE)
+ 3.00 MEGASECONDS

A raid. While he, Raul Nakamore, had been chasing the phantom Ship from Outside, it had run literal rings around him and raided the very distillery his borrowed ships had been set to defend. While he was still locked into his initial—futile—trajectory toward Lansing, without fuel enough to make an attempt at further pursuit anything but a joke. Raul drummed irritably on the arm of his seat, having no better way to vent his frustration.

And yet, the reports he'd received indicated that the starship had not headed directly out of the system, indicated, in fact, that the ship might be tracking his own course and returning again to Lansing. Raul glanced at the instrument board, seeing twenty-seven hundred kiloseconds elapsed, only twenty-three kiloseconds remaining before they reached Lansing. Like the fable of the tortoise and the hare—slowed by the stolen hydrogen, the starship would never reach Lansing before them, if Lansing was its destination. But why should it be? Why would these outsiders play pirate for Lansing, when they'd suffered losses in the Rings already? Revenge? But they could easily have destroyed the distillery, and instead they stole one thousand tons of hydrogen: too little to cripple the Grand Harmony, too much for a ramscoop's drive.

And showing them how to steal it had been Wadie

Abdhiamal . . . Wadie Abdhiamal of the Demarchy. Outlawed by the Demarchy, Djem had said, voted a traitor by his own people for helping the starship escape them. And if there was one thing he, Raul, was sure of, it was that Abdhiamal was no traitor. Why had he betrayed the future of his own people, then? He might not be a jingoist but he wasn't insane. Why would he threaten Snows-of-Salvation, when he knew better than any other demarch what it meant to the survival of both their peoples? Why would he betray his friends? Because they had been his friends; and by betraying them he had cut himself off from the only haven he would have found in his exile.

Maybe he'd been forced into it. But Djem hadn't thought that Abdhiamal had acted like a man who had been forced. . . . Raul knew that Djem would never forgive Wadie Abdhiamal—for the betrayal of their friendship, if for no other reason. What was it about that ship, or whoever ran it, that would make a man like Abdhiamal willing to sacrifice everything? Maybe he would never know. But if that ship was following them to Lansing . . .

Raul stretched and turned to look at Sandoval. Sandoval sat with an expression of uncompromising boredom on his hawk-nosed profile, rereading a novel tape. A good officer, Raul thought. If he believed this use of his ship and crew was fruitless or pointless, he never let it show. Raul kept his own doubts and speculations private. Twenty-three kiloseconds to Lansing. And maybe they wouldn't be disappointed after all. . . .

The sight of Discus, shrunken almost to insignificance, greeted Raul as he pushed off from the hatch, drifting down to the stony surface of Lansing's docking field. He remembered looking up into a Demarchy sky, long ago, where Discus had been only a bright starpoint, one of a thousand scattered stars, and as unreachable as the stars. He remembered the feeling of isolation and desolation that had struck him then. But this time, invisible now but much closer at hand, there was the ship that he had left in low orbit above Lansing to ensure their safety. He moved cautiously as he waited for the handful of crew from the two docked ships, easing tension and unused muscles; grateful, after nearly three megaseconds, for the return of normal gravity. Across the field lay three other ships. He studied them with a fleeting curiosity, realizing that even Lansing had the nuclear-electric rockets that the Grand Harmony didn't have; but realizing too that these ships were so deadly that even the Harmony would be better off without them. Below him (the angle of gravity's feeble drag put the term into his mind), the semitransparent plastic that shrouded nine-tenths of Lansing rock showed muted patched of green and gold, pastelled by the angle of his sight. He thought of drifted snow, the pastels of impure gases crystallized by cold.

This was Lansing, the once-proud capital of a once-proud Heaven Belt, the only world of its kind. Its self-contained ecosystem had recreated Old Earth, and that was why its population had survived the war; and because, as a capital, it had been a showplace and nothing more. He knew that Lansing had been reduced to piracy at the time of their last close pass with Discus; he wondered what they had been reduced to by now. His crew were nervous and hostile. He had given orders for them to remain suited even inside the asteroid, to isolate them from any contagion—and to isolate them from any other incidents that might come out of a face-to-face confrontation with the locals.

They started toward the single airlock visible in the hillside above the ships. Raul glanced on up at the solitary radio antenna on the crest of the naked hill. It was half-illuminated by the cold light of the distant sun, sinking into shadow as the planetoid tumbled endlessly, imperceptibly. No lights blinked along its slender stalk as a warning to docking ships. His radioman had been unable to detect any broadcast response from Lansing. He wondered whether their communications had failed entirely, whether they even knew his ships had landed . . . whether–like an unpleasant premonition–they might all be dead.

One of his men turned the wheel on the hatchway sunk into the rock; he watched it begin to cycle. The men behind him waited, without eagerness, without relief, without any sense of triumph at having reached their goal. He heard only broken whispers, an uneasy muttering, picked up by his suit radio. Their silence surprised him until he realized that it was an extension of his own; as if isolation and the pall of death that shrouded the Main Belt like a tent shrouded this world had affected them all. The airlock hatch swung out. With a sudden vision of the yawning pit, the gates of hell, Raul entered the underworld.

The lock cycled again, replacing vacuum with atmosphere in the crowded space between. Raul felt his suit lose its armor rigidity, glanced back to be sure that no one disobeyed him by loosening a helmet. After nearly three megaseconds of uncertain reprocessed air, he knew well enough how strong the temptation was. He checked his rifle, settled it in the crook of his arm.

The inner hatch slid open. He looked through–into the staring faces of half a dozen men and women, frozen in disbelief. They had not, he gathered, been expecting him. He pushed through into the corridor, searching the frightened faces for a sign of leadership;

taking in the filth, the patched and piecemeal clothing. He heard the startled curses of the men behind him, raised his own voice. "All right, who—"

A woman who might have been young or old moved away from the rest toward him, carrying something bundled in rags; he saw a sheen of tears filming her cheeks, her dark eyes fixed on him with peculiar urgency. He heard her voice, trembling, ". . . a miracle, it's a miracle . . ." Before he could react she had forced the bundle into his arms; she pushed off and disappeared down the sloping tunnel. Taken aback, he looked down at the ragged bundle and found himself holding a newborn child. The baby made no sound; when he saw why, he turned his face away. "Whose baby is this?" His voice hardened with anger, with denial.

One of the men moved toward him, fear still on his face, a kind of desperation dragging him forward. "It's mine . . . ours. Please . . . please, let me have it." Something in his tone made the baby a thing. He stretched his arms; one sleeve flopped free, torn up to the elbow. His nails were outlined with black dirt; dirt filigreed the lines of his hands.

Raul held the child out slowly, uncertain. The father took it, almost jerked it from his arms. Abruptly the man pushed through the circle of armed crewmen and caught the edge of the hatchway. He thrust the baby inside, his hand found the control plate, his fist struck it and started it cycling.

Raul saw Sandoval leap forward, but the man pressed himself against the wall, covering the plate, as the door began to slide shut. Sandoval's gloved fist caught him by the front of his shirt, ripping the rotten cloth; the man pushed him away with a foot. The hatch sealed shut as Sandoval tried to force his fingers into the gap. The light blinked red from green above their heads. "Why you—" Sandoval turned back, as two of his crew pinned the man between them.

"Sandoval!" Raul raised a hand. "That's enough. That's enough. . . . It was a—mercy killing. Let him go."

"Sir—" He saw Sandoval's rage trapped behind helmet glass.

Raul shook his head, putting aside the memory of his own three daughters and two sons, all grown now and sound. He watched the father sag against the wall in slow motion as the crewmen released him. The man plucked mournfully at the drifting edges of his torn shirt, as though the tear were a death wound.

Raul glanced back down the tunnel, saw that the rest of the onlookers had disappeared. He moved toward their prisoner through the crew's muttered anger, through a ring of set faces. The man cringed and put up his hands, "I had to . . . I had to. Somebody had to do it; she knew that, but she wouldn't admit it! Everybody said so. It would've died anyway—wouldn't it? Wouldn't it? You saw it, it was defective. . . ." He lowered his hands, reached out to grasp Raul's suited arm, "You saw it?"

Raul's fist tightened against the urge to slap the hand away. He took a deep breath. "Yes, I saw it. It wouldn't have lived."

The man began to whimper, clinging to his sleeve. "Thank you . . . thank you . . ."

Raul shook him roughly, caught somewhere between pity and disgust. "Who are you?"

The man looked at him blankly, stupidly.

"Your name," Raul said. "Identify yourself."

"Wind . . . Wind Kitavu." The man straightened, letting go of Raul's arm as reason came back into his eyes; aged eyes in a young man's face. "Who—what are you doin' here?"

"Askin' the questions. First, is anybody in charge here, and if so, can you take us to 'em?"

Wind Kitavu nodded, staring distractedly into the muzzles of half a dozen rifles. "The prime minister, the Assembly. I know where the chambers are. I'll take you. . . ." His fingers searched the tear in his shirt again, drew the edges together nervously. "You aren't the—" Raul watched the question form on his lips, saw him swallow it. "You want me to take you?"

Raul gestured his men aside; letting Wind Kitavu pass, he followed, and the crewmen fell in behind him. He noticed that one of the prisoner's legs was shorter than the other and twisted. *The gates of hell; the capital of Heaven.*

They were not led out onto the surface as he had expected. Wind Kitavu kept to the subterranean hallways, where dull-eyed men and women with stringy hair watched them pass, showing mingled fear and wonder, but mostly showing confusion. *No threat.* He felt his warinesss settle into a bleak feeling of depression. A woman pushed out from the wall, moving with Wind Kitavu, ". . . starship . . .?" Wind Kitavu shook his head, and she drifted free, her face tightening. Raul saw despair in her eyes as he passed, and his spirits rose.

On his orders Wind Kitavu pointed the way to the communications center, and he sent Sandoval with two men to investigate. With the others he continued on, wondering what they would find when they reached the assembly chambers.

Whatever he had been expecting could not have prepared him for what he found. Someone had sent word of their arrival ahead: seven figures stood waiting, tiny in a vast rough-walled chamber that he somehow instinctively knew must have been intended for storage and not as a meeting hall. And like gem crystals in a matrix of barren rock, the five men and two women shone, resplendent in robes of state. One man, Raul noticed, was still adjusting the folds of a sleeve tangled by haste. The nearest of them started forward, his drifting progress a ceremony, his face set in expressionless formality. Raul studied the intricacies of layer on layer of brocade as the official approached: the fibers absorbed and enhanced light, sent it back at his eyes in a shower of scintillating fire. He began to see, as he probed the wash of gemlight, the patches where it dimmed and faltered. The garments were stained and frayed, eaten by time. The man wore a soft, turbaned head covering of the same material; his seamed face and gnarled hands, fading darkly against the brilliance, were clean.

Raul waited silently until the official reached him. The six assembly members, their own threadbare splendor muted, clustered slowly behind him. Their group stare rested on Raul's weapon rather than his face. At last the man lifted his gaze, searching Raul's helmet glass to meet his eyes. "I am Silver Tyr,"—the voice surprised him with its unwitting arrogance—"President of the Lansing Assembly, Prime Minister of the Heaven Belt—"

The man broke off, as laughter rattled in Raul's helmet; for a long second he didn't realize that it was not his own bitten-off laugh, that it had come from one of his crewmen. He raised a hand to stop it, hearing mentally the clattering mockery the chamber would make of the sound.

"And you are—?" The prime minister forced the words with rigid dignity—demanding respect not for an aging shadow man, ludicrous in the rags of lost richness, but for the undeniable fact of the lost dream-time, of what they had all been, once, before their fall from grace.

"Raul Nakamore, Hand of Harmony." And almost unthinkingly he held out a hand, gloved against contamination but open in friendship, in recognition. "We mean you people no harm; we only want your cooperation while we're here."

The prime minister extended a hand, wtih the hesitancy of a man who expected to have it lopped off. "And what have you come here for, sir?"

Raul shook the hand, let it go, before he answered. "We've come huntin' pirates, Your Excellency." He dredged the unaccustomed title up from a half-forgotten history lesson. He noted the ill-concealed start of guilty knowledge on more than one face.

Seeing him observe it, the prime minister said, almost protesting, "But that happened almost a gigasec ago, Hand Nakamore—and it was an act of need, as you must know. Surely you haven't come all this way, after all this time, to punish—"

"I'm not speakin' of your last raid on the Rings, Your Excellency—I think you know that. I'm speakin' of a starship from outside the Heaven system, that destroyed one of our Navy craft and raided our main distillery—and is passin' by Lansing on its way out of this system—"

"Sir—" Raul heard Sandoval's voice, turned at the sound of more men entering the room.

Sandoval and the two crewmen joined his group, escorting an angry, thin-faced woman. Brown skin, brown eyes, brown hair graying at the temples: Raul assessed her as she assessed him. He felt her anger flick out in a lash of wordless contempt as she glanced at the robed figures of the assembly. Her gaze returned to him, the anger cooling; he thought of a fire banked, controlled, still burning underneath.

"Sir, we found this woman in the radio room. She claims their comm's out of order."

He nodded; turned back as the prime minister said, "We know nothin' about a starship. You saw the only ships we've got. They can't even reach Discus any more—"

"Face reality, Silver Tyr!" The sharp edge of the woman's voice slashed his words. "He can see you're lyin'; all of you, you couldn't cover the truth any more than those robes cover your rags. If he didn't know the truth before, he knows it now. The best we can do is cooperate, the way he says, and hope maybe he'll be willin' to bargain—"

"Flame Siva! Would you betray the only people in the universe who care enough to help us? And your own daughter—"

"No cripple, no defective, is a child of mine." Her voice betrayed her. Raul felt the heat of bitter disappointment in the ashes of her words. The sagging figure of crippled Wind Kitavu tightened in a flinch. "But that's irrelevant, anyway, under the circumstances."

A frown settled into the lines of the prime minister's face. "Two of our people are on board the starship. They say the Grand Harmony attacked the starship first. It has a reason and a right to retaliate against you, and you have no legal claim on it, in our judgment. We have no intention of cooperatin' with any attempt to seize it."

"I see." Raul matched the frown, realizing that there was nothing he could really do to these people, because he had already destroyed their only hope. "Fortunately for you, we don't really need your cooperation . . . but we won't tolerate any interference. We intend to wait here until that ship arrives." He studied their responses; knew, with certainty and a kind of callous joy, that it would. "One of my ships is remainin' in orbit above Lansing; if we encounter any resistance, the captain has orders to hole your tent. If you want what time you've got left to you, don't get in our way."

"Even on Lansing we don't run to meet Death, Hand Nakamore." The prime minister looked down at his gun.

"Especially on Lansing," Flame Siva said. "We're Materialists, Hand Nakamore, realists. At least we're supposed to be." She paused. "Just what are you plannin' to do to that ship and its crew? Will you seize it intact?"

Raul laughed shortly. "That's what we'll try to do. But I'd disable it permanently before I'd let it get away from us again. And we want the crew alive, to show us how to run it. But if they refuse to let us board—piracy is a high crime by anybody's law, punishable by death." He saw the assembly members shift, glittering.

"She's lost most of her crew to you already," the woman murmured, almost to the floor.

"She?" Raul said, surprised. "That's right"—remembering a detail of alienness and the detection of human remains—"she: a woman pilot. So her crew is shorthanded?"

"Two of our own people are with them," she repeated. He realized that it was more than a simple statement of fact: *her daughter*, the prime minister had said. Her hand rose, agitated; she brushed her neck, her matted hair, controlling a gesture he recognized as threatening. "The captain promised us the hydrogen we need to survive, if they helped her get it for her own ship . . . the hydrogen you wouldn't share with either of us, unless we took it from you by force."

He waited, not responding because she hadn't made it a challenge.

"What would you give us if I helped you secure the ship intact?"

Surprised again, he asked, "What could you do to guarantee that?"

Thin hands crossed before her, locked around her thin arms; sleeves that were too long and too wide slid back. "Allow me to finish repairs on the radio . . . give me parts for it if you have them." She glanced up, her eyes hard and bright. "Let me make contact with the ship when it approaches, to reassure them that it's safe to come in close, so that you can take them easily."

"We could do that ourselves."

"No, you can't. My—our people on the ship know the radio here and its problems, and they know my voice. A stranger's voice would make them suspect somethin' was wrong . . . and so would radio silence."

"You may have a point." Raul nodded.

"Will you leave us the hydrogen if I do that?" No fire showed this time.

"If the ship escapes, they can come back with the hydrogen!" Wind Kitavu burst out. "Don't take away our only chance—"

She turned; her face silenced him. Raul wondered what showed on it. She turned back. "Will you?"

Knowing how easy it would be to lie, he said, "I'll request permission. Maybe I'll get it; maybe I won't." He waited for her reaction, was puzzled by a kind of exasperation, as if she had wanted him to lie, wanted an excuse to perform treason. Or was it something else? He thought of Wadie Abdhiamal.

"But the crew, then? If you . . . take the ship intact."

"If I take them alive?" *Her daughter* . . . finding in that sufficient explanation at last. "So she does matter to you?"

Flame Siva started; her eyes were cinders, her voice lost its strength. "Yes . . . of course she matters. . . ." And suddenly defiant, "They all matter! They're tryin' to save us!" She stopped, biting her lip.

Raul shifted lightly. "If they don't resist us, we'll release your daughter and the other one here; if that's what you want." *That'll be punishment enough.* "For the rest—there's a Demarchy traitor on board, who gave 'em the information to hit our distillery. I don't think he's left himself much of an option." *But I still want an explanation.* "And the outsider crew, what's left of it—they'll cooperate with our navy, one way or another, I expect."

"You'll never let them go." Not a question.

"I don't think either the crew or our navy will ever be in a position to negotiate about that."

She nodded, or shook her head, a peculiar sideward motion. "We do what we can, here . . . and take what we can get. We're responsible for our own actions." Again the defiance, the spite, the fire . . . she faced the ghosts incarnate of the Lansing assembly. "We take the consequences."

"Sandoval." Raul signaled him forward. "Take her back, let her work on the radio. And whatever happens, don't let her broadcast anythin', repeat, *any*thin', until you get the word from me."

"Yes, sir." Sandoval saluted smoothly and led her away, her head high, flanked by guards.

Raul delegated two more men to guard the airlock, keeping one with him. The prime minister and the assembly members waited, aware once more—as he was aware—of their lack of consequence, their loss of control.

The prime minister turned to Wind Kitavu, his robes opening like a blossom. "You. What are you doin' down here like this?"

"You know what I was doin'." Wind Kitavu jerked into an arc away from the wall. "The baby. You all know, don't act like you didn't!"

The prime minister drew back, an undignified motion. "Then don't expect anythin' from us! You knew what would happen. Accept your own mistakes . . . get back to work." He stretched his arm.

Raul saw dirt still crusting it from wrist to elbow as his sleeve moved. He heard one of his crewmen laugh out loud again, seeing it; did nothing this time to check it. He turned away. "Wind Kitavu."

Wind Kitavu halted his sullen drift toward the door.

"Are you goin' out onto the surface?"

A nod, faceless. "Got to tell my—wife. Tell her about the baby."

"Then we'll follow you up. I want to see those damned gardens."

"Damned gardens . . ." It echoed, someone else's voice; Wind Kitavu moved toward the exit. Raul did not turn back to acknowledge the Prime Minister of all Heaven Belt.

Raul followed his unresponsive guide through more tunnels, this time feeling the upward slant. Brightness grew from a point of light ahead of him, widening as he rose to meet it—an intensity of light that could only be the sun's. But this time he approached day in the way that had been natural for the human species through the countless years of its existence, a way that for him was entirely novel and unexpected: he crossed into the daylight freely, easily, unhindered by any barrier.

And stopped, absorbing, absorbed by the blinding greenness that enfolded him as he emerged from the hillside. He had a sudden, vivid memory of the hydroponics greenhouses of the Harmony, the heat and humidity that made them a sweltering hell to the average citizen. His crewman retreated into the tunnel's entrance behind him; he ordered him back sharply. Periodic hydroponics service was required of all citizens, a shared trial. He had done hydroponics service in his youth; but as a Hand of Harmony, it was no longer required of him. *Maybe rank does have its privileges.*

But the handful of ragged workers clustering now didn't look any more uncomfortable than the ones in the tunnels behind him. Insulated by his suit, he would never experience the reality of the gardens, of how life had been on Old Earth. Two futures waited here with him, in the balance of life and death—and either way, he would never have this opportunity again. . . .

He looked back at the shifting knot of sullen, dirty faces, at the genetic deformities that marked them like a brand. Above them all, latticed and embroidered by the fragile looming trees, the roof of the sky was a transparent membrane, disfigured too by blotches of clumsy patchwork. Once there must have been something more, a shield of force to protect them from solar radiation . . . a protection that had long since been lost. In the Grand Harmony permanent hydroponics duty was given as a punishment. Here it was a punishment too, in a different way; for the crime of having been a victim. . . . He left his helmet on, the idea of contamination back in his mind again: not the contamination of disease but a more pernicious contamination of the spirit. It was not a place he wanted to get the feel of, after all.

"What is it now?" One of them clutched at Wind Kitavu's sleeve, pulling his torn shirt halfway off his shoulder. "Are they wearin' *suits* to come out an' preach at us now?"

Wind Kitavu worked free, jerking his shirt back up his arm. "No . . ." His voice dropped, his hand gestured at them as he explained. Raul lost the words as an atmosphere in gentle motion hissed sibilance. He watched the lithe motion of the reaching trees, watched an expression that was growing too familiar spread from face to face in the group of workers, the desolation so complete that it could not even re-form into anger.

Wind Kitavu asked something in return, and the man who had stopped him pointed vaguely away. Without asking permission, without turning even to look back, Wind Kitavu left them, disappearing between the shrubs, loosening a slow shower of pastel blossom petals where he passed. *The baby.* Raul made no move to stop him, remembering what it was he went to do and having no desire to be a witness to it. The other workers began to drift back and away, still watching him warily as their bare feet pushed off from the springy mat of trampled vegetation.

Raul glanced back into the tunnel, still empty behind him. He noticed for the first time that the overhead lamps that illuminated the underground were flameless. Electricity . . . somewhere these people still had a functioning generator, probably an atomic battery from before the war—or even from some later trade with the Demarchy. He considered again the fact that the Grand Harmony had none at all because of the Demarchy. If not for their bounty of snow, the Grand Harmony would be in a worse position than Lansing—and the only worse position was death.

The Demarchy made him think of Wadie Abdhiamal and the mystery that lay behind their impending meeting. He had seen Abdhiamal function as a negotiator at Snows-of-Salvation: inexperienced, unsure of his own position, but wringing cooperation out of both sides with an instinct for fairness that dissolved cultural biases the way a heated knife sank through an ice block. And as a ship's captain he had transported Abdhiamal to meetings in Central Harmony and half the inhabited rocks of the Rings. He had seen the man ignored, insulted, actively threatened, but never losing patience. . . . And he had been surprised, suspicious, and finally pleased when Abdhiamal questioned him about matters of Harmony governmental policy. Pleased, in the end, because he saw Abdhiamal actually listen and learn and make use of what he learned to help them all.

The only weakness he had found in Wadie Abdhiamal was his inability to deal with one thing—the inevitability of Heaven's end. He had found that Abdhiamal believed some answer still existed; while he, Raul, like the people of Lansing, had seen long ago that the only answer was death. And yet he began to suspect that Abdhiamal's obsessive optimism covered a conviction as certain as his own that Heaven was doomed . . . but more than that, it covered a deep, pathological fear: Abdhiamal was not a man who could accept that all he accomplished would mean nothing in the end. He could not continue on that road, knowing its end was in sight; he would stumble and fall, crushed by the burden of his own knowledge. And so some part of Abdhiamal's mind had shut the truth away, buried it in a lie that let him continue. Raul had envied Abdhiamal the Demarchy, where comparative richness helped him protect his illusions. And he had wondered whether anything would ever force him to admit the truth. . . .

But the starship—even he, Raul, had discovered hope again in what it could offer Heaven . . . and, specifically, the Grand Harmony. Why would Abdhiamal, of all people, try to make sure that neither of their governments got its hands on the ship? Abdhiamal was a fair man—but was he fair to the point of insanity, of genocide? And the woman who piloted the ship . . . why would she run such risks to keep a promise to a place like Lansing? Were they both insane, were they all? Or was there something he wasn't seeing? . . . Too many things that he couldn't see. But *if* she kept her promise, if that ship was falling right into his hands . . . that was the only answer that he would ever need. Ever.

RANGER (LANSING SPACE) + 3.09 MEGASECONDS

"Can't you raise Lansing, Pappy?" Betha moved stiffly up from the rendezvous program on the control board.

Clewell pulled the ear jack wearily away from his head. "No. I've got the ship monitoring all up and down the spectrum. If anyone talks to us we'll hear it."

"Maybe the transmitter broke down," Shadow Jack said. "It's out about half the time, seems like. They have a hard time keepin' it repaired." Bird Alyn floated beside him above Betha's head, gazing at the magnified image of Lansing on the screen. Betha watched the cloudy, marshmallow softness of the tent passing below: a shroud for a dying people, who would live a little longer because of the *Ranger*.

Discus hung above and to the left, tilted and indistinct, a tiny finger's jewel. And somewhere in the closer darkness: three fusion ships from the Demarchy. Not one of them had begun deceleration to match velocities with Lansing and the *Ranger*. Their mission was one of murder. . . . Betha glanced at the latest tracking update; less than ten minutes left to offload the hydrogen.

"Well, our time is a little limited . . . I'm sure that Lansing won't mind if we drop you and the tanks into low orbit, and then get ourselves out of here." She smiled up at Shadow Jack and Bird Alyn, forcing warmth into her voice. "They should be glad to see you two coming home with eight hundred tons of hydrogen."

"They will," Shadow Jack said. They nodded, their faces shining clean and smiling bravely above the collars of their pressure suits. "But . . . are you sure you're goin' to be all right when we go?" An odd longing edged his voice, and a secret shame. "Just the–two of you?" He glanced away at Clewell's drawn face, cracking his knuckles.

From the corner of her eye Betha saw Wadie look at her . . . impeccable Abdhiamal, in embroidered jacket and faded dungarees. She smiled in spite of her self. "We'll be all right," she said, managing a confidence her own aching, battered body did not really believe, for his sake. She would not play on his guilt to make him change his mind. They had come this far; they would find a way to do the rest, somehow. Later . . . she'd think about it later. "Don't crack your knuckles, Shadow Jack. You'll ruin your joints."

Shadow Jack grinned feebly and stuffed his hands into his gloves.

Wadie touched her shoulder. "Look."

As they spoke the *Ranger* had slipped a quarter of the way around Lansing. On the near horizon, they saw a blunt protrusion of naked stone, the tent lapping its slope like clouds below a mountaintop.

"The Mountain," Bird Alyn said. "There're the radio–antennas, an' the moorage . . . there's one of our–"

"Hey." Shadow Jack tugged at her arm. "That's not one of our ships! I never saw anythin' like that; where'd it come from?"

"Maybe it's salvage."

"No, look, there's another one."

Betha increased the magnification. "Pappy, those look like–"

"–Ringers! Ringers, go back, it's a trap, a–" A woman's voice burst out of the speaker, was choked off.

"Mother!" A small cry escaped from Bird Alyn.

"Those look like chemical rockets down there." Clewell finished the sentence, his voice like dry leaves rattling.

Wadie's hand tightened on her shoulder. "My God, those are Ringer ships; fifty million kilometers from Discus. . . ." His voice sharpened with disbelief. "The Demarchy knew the Harmony had a couple of high-mass-ratio strike forces, but nothin' like this. To be here now, with only chemical rockets, they must've started right after they first attacked you. And even then they'd need a mass ratio of a thousand to one–"

A new voice came over the speaker: "Outsider starship! This is Hand Nakamore of the Grand Harmony. Maintain your present orbit. Do not activate your drive or you'll be fired upon. One of my ships will approach you now for boarding." Betha looked down on the airless mountain, at three cumbersome Ringer craft, each hardly more than a mass of propellant tanks surrounding a tiny crew module. At last she saw one of them begin to rise, its invisible backwash kicking up clouds of surface rubble. *Trapped. . . .* Her hands knotted at her sides. The best the *Ranger* could ever do was one gravity; and now she could only get one-quarter of that, with the load strapped to its hull. The Ringer chemical rockets could do several gees for more than long enough to close with them.

The seconds passed; the Ringer ship rose slowly, almost insolently, toward them. The minutes passed . . . and with them, the *Ranger*'s last hope of avoiding the Demarchy fleet as well. *Christ, why must we lose now, when we're so close!*

Wadie hooked a foot under the rail along the panel,

steadying himself. "Betha, that was Djem Nakamore's half-brother, Raul, on the radio. He's a Hand of Harmony, an officer in their navy. A high-ranking officer. Let me talk to him. He probably knows what I did at Snows-of-Salvation, but we were friends, once."

"Better wait, Abdhiamal," Clewell said quietly. "We've got more company, sophisticated wideband." He touched a switch and another segment of the screen brightened.

"Lije MacWong," Wadie said; Betha saw the easy grace tighten out of his body.

"Captain Torgussen: If you're receiving this, you must realize that the Demarchy has pursued your ship. The distance-velocity gap between us is small enough now so that you can't outrun our missiles; do not attempt to leave Lansing space." Behind MacWong's self-satisfied face Betha could see a control room half the size of the *Ranger*'s and a ship's officer in a sun-gold jacket. Farther back in the room she saw cameras trained on the screen, saw a cluster of demarchs, like bright-painted wooden dolls—company representatives overseeing their interests. She saw Esrom Tiriki, felt her mouth tighten.

She signaled at Clewell to transmit. "I hear you, MacWong. And I'm impressed. Have you actually come all this way just to destroy my ship? You can't take us now; all you can do is destroy us in passing. . . ." She hesitated. MacWong's startling blue eyes still stared blindly from the screen. She realized, chagrined, that even closing at eight hundred kilometers per second the Demarchy ships were still millions of kilometers away; light itself took half a minute to bridge the gap.

At last MacWong reacted, looked past her to Wadie. For an instant she saw apology and regret; another second, and she saw only triumph. "On the contrary, Captain Torgussen. We have no intention of destroyin' your starship—if you obey our instructions. Our ships will pass through your vicinity in about four thousand seconds. You have that much time to dismantle and deactivate your drive. If, by that time, you haven't satisfactorily proved that your ship will be immobilized till we return for it, you will be fired on and destroyed. The people want your ship intact, Captain, but if they can't have it, they don't intend to let it go to anybody else."

Betha pushed back, her arms rigid against the panel. "Wadie . . . he's no fool after all." The *Ranger* lay in the jaws of a trap; and each jaw was unaware of the other. When the jaws closed on her ship, they would have to destroy each other too. She let go of the panel, forcing a smile. "Then I'm afraid you have a problem too, MacWong. We would have been gone before you arrived, except that someone else is already holding us here . . . Hand Nakamore, I'm sure you've been monitoring. Would you care to comment?" She waited, savoring the bitterness of useless satisfaction.

Clewell grunted. "The Ringers are transmitting video, not to be outdone. . . ." A new patch of screen brightened with a black-and-white image. The Ringer control room was small, the crew strapped down to padded couches crowded by equipment: an image from the earliest days of space travel. A thickset Belter in a helmet with the Discan rings for insignia sat nearest the camera, his face grim behind a stubble of beard. "This is Hand Nakamore of the Grand Harmony. My forces have seized the Outsider starship, and if it attempts to comply with your demands, we'll destory it. We have several prewar fusion bombs in our possession. If you attempt to keep us from takin' that ship we'll do our damnedest to destroy you too."

Betha glanced at Wadie, questioning.

"He could have the bonbs; salvage from the war."

Wadie studied the embroidered whorls on his jacket front. "If he could maneuver into MacWong's path with them, he wouldn't have to be too accurate, even if it took the Demarchy crews a megasec to die of radiation poisoning. Things like this happened during the war, crews of dead men fighting their final battle. That's how we got three fusion craft intact. . . ." He raised his eyes. "Nakamore will never let the Demarchy take the *Ranger*, even if it means he has to die too."

Betha saw the trace of consternation that betrayed MacWong at the sight of Nakamore; the obvious disbelief on the ruddy face of the ship's officer and on the face of Esrom Tiriki. She watched them change again to hatred and defiance, heard MacWong begin an angry response.

"And so we're all going to die, and so are they . . . and so is Heaven." Her voice rose. "And for what? This is insane—"

"Don't you think they know that?" Wadie moved toward her, almost touched her again. "They know it as well as we do. But they're trapped here just as we are; all that's happened in the last two and a half gigasecs since the war, all the frustration and fear, has been leadin' down to this. . . . It had to end like this. Your own song says it—'No one ever changed a world.' "

She drew away from him. "It's the people who have to be willing to change! It didn't have to end like this. If they could have seen that there was still a future . . . There could still be one now, but even you can't see it; you won't see it. You're right, death *is* what you want. . . . Suicide is the ultimate selfishness, and I've never seen a people more ready to commit it." She unstrapped, pushing up out of her seat and away from him, her breath catching at the punishment of sudden movement. "You deserve it. Damn you all!"

He caught her wrist. Furious, she felt Shadow Jack move out of her way, staring, as Wadie pulled her back to the screen. "MacWong, Raul, this in Abdhiamal. I want to talk to you."

Nakamore acknowledged him and Betha thought she saw a smile; she waited, saw MacWong break off his speech: "Sorry, Abdhiamal. You're a dead man. You've got nothin' to say to the Demarchy." MacWong glanced sideways, barely turning his head. Betha looked past him at Tiriki.

"We're all dead men unless you listen to me! Be cause of this ship, which you don't have any more right to than Nakamore does, or I do. For God's sake, MacWong, there were seven people on this ship, who came three light-years from another system to Heaven; and five of them are already dead because of it. And now you're goin' to destroy the rest of them, along with the best ships left to the Demarchy and the Rings? You're all that's left of Heaven Belt, and your own greed is ripping your guts out. You're killin' yourselves because you're scared to die. Taking the starship won't save Heaven, and it's goin' to finish you off instead, if you let it.

"But you don't have to let it happen." He nodded at Betha waiting beside him, silent with surprise. "These people came to trade with us because they wanted a better life. And in spite of what we've done to them, they're still willin' to trade. There's a whole trade ring of worlds out there, holding each other up so that they never fall into the kind of trap we've put ourselves in. They can save us too. Heaven Belt can be all it ever was if we join them." He waited, search ing the screen for a response. "Let the starship leave Heaven, instead of destroyin' it. You'll accomplish the same goal but you'll have everything to gain and nothing to lose."

"You always could convince Djem that cold was hot, Wadie." Betha looked for mockery on Nakamore's face, was surprised when she didn't find it. "But this time you even make sense to me. . . . I don't *want* to destroy the starship or my own ships. If I could get out of this bind by lettin' the ship leave the system, I would. The way things have turned out, it'd be enough just to put the ship beyond everybody's reach. . . . And the point's not lost on me that the only reason we've got you now is that this woman, this Captain Torgussen, came back to Lansing as she said she would." Nakamore found Betha's eyes, curiously respectful. "I think you would come back to help us too."

Betha frowned in sudden pain, bit her lip.

"I'm willin' to let you go, Captain. But is MacWong?"

Betha saw MacWong surreptitiously rolling the lace on his shirt front, still listening to Nakamore's transmission. Behind him the mediamen transmitted his own every move, his every word, to the waiting Demarchy: MacWong was pinned under the public gaze like a bug under glass. At last he said, "Your suggestion violates the Demarchy's mandate for this mission. I only have the authority to seize the ship or destroy it; I can't let it go."

"Even though you want to! Even though we may all die if you don't." Nakamore's words burned with contempt; his taciturn face was abruptly transformed, as though he were making a speech. Betha realized suddenly that he must be well aware that there was an audience waiting to receive it. Wadie began to smile, almost wonderingly. "You puppet. You call the Harmony a 'dictatorship' but we give more freedom to the individual than your people's mobocracy ever did or will. I have the power, the freedom of choice, to stop this stupidity. But you don't. Your people don't trust a man to use the judgment he was born with; they pick the words every time you open your mouth.

"But how are they goin' to tell you what to do this time, MacWong? They never imagined needing second-to-second control over hundreds of millions of kilometers, across a comm lag like this. By the time the whole Demarchy hears this and debates and amends and votes, things will be all over for us, and whatever they wanted won't mean a damn thing. . . . But you won't take the decision in your own hands because you're too afraid of the system, and of those pretty-boy anarchists behind you. The basic weakness and inefficiency of your self-servin' mob rule will make the Demarchy destroy its own ships, and mine, and destroy this system's last hope of survival. I've always known your 'government' was a farce . . . an' even you can't deny that now. I'd laugh if it wasn't such a tragedy. Because that's what it is, a tragedy."

Betha watched impotent rage fracture MacWong's mask of complacency, saw real emotion for the first time on the faces of the listening demarchs behind hmi . . . saw the mediamen recording it all, so that the entire Demarchy could see and share their indignation. MacWong covered his anger. "Captain Torgussen, our ships will pass you in thirty-six hundred seconds. If you intend to follow our instructions, I suggest you get in touch with us soon." His image vanished abruptly.

Betha said softly, "Try to monitor MacWong's communications with the Demarchy, Pappy; let me know how much worse that outbursts makes things."

Nakamore loosened the upturned collar of his stiff, bulky jacket, the anger flowing out of his eyes and voice. "He'll be back, I expect."

"My congratulations on . . . your promotion to Hand, Raul." Betha watched Wadie bow, inscrutable.

"My duty, to accept; my desire, to serve." Nakamore gestured the honor aside, oddly embrarassed. "I wish I could say the same to you, Wadie. But I don't know the Demarchy's etiquette for its traitors."

Wadie smiled bleakly. "There's not any."

"You're the only reasonable demarch I ever met, and that's probably why the mob went after you. I don't approve of your act of piracy against the Harmony . . . but I think I finally begin to see why you did it; why you want to help these people. I doubt if Djem'll ever understand it—"

"I know . . . and I'm sorry. There wasn't any other choice. It would never have happened if—"

"If we hadn't attacked the starship when it first appeared? You're right. It was stupid of us. If we'd had sense enough to direct 'em to one of our bases instead, the Grand Harmony'd have its own starship now. But we didn't, and all we got was death. But we knew the ship was damaged, and Central Harmony figured it was worth the gamble I could catch them here."

"That was a long chance," Wadie said. "You'd have been a long time gettin' home if what we saw is all the propellant you've got left."

"I know. Even without a battle, it would take us twenty megasecs to get back to Outermost—if our life-support systems held out. And then we'd freeze our asses off on that snowball, waitin' for a fuel shipment to get us to the inner Harmony." Nakamore scratched his chin, looking tired. "But we took on food and air down on Lansing."

Shadow Jack pushed past Betha's shoulder to the camera. "Why didn't you just rip the tent and kill 'em quick, you bastard?"

Nakamore shrugged. "Boy, you're all pirates to me.

But we didn't take that much. Look on it as a trade for the hydrogen you stole from the Harmony."

"Where's my mother?" Bird Alyn cried suddenly, shrill with anguish. "What did you do to my mother?"

Nakamore peered at her blankly; Betha saw comprehension come to him. "So . . . your mother's goin' to have a stiff jaw for a few hundred kilosecs. But aside from that she's better off than you are—or we are—right now. Speakin' of which: Captain Torgussen, you have my permission to offload those gas canisters into a low orbit around Lansing. Then I recommend all our ships move out a few hundred kilometers into space. When the Demarchy forces arrive the fireworks'll be lethal over quite a volume; there's no reason why Lansing should be part of it. Somebody might as well get somethin' out of this." He turned away, issuing soundless orders.

"Thank you," Betha said. She saw the curious smile still on Wadie's face as he watched the screen. "What is that man? I don't understand him."

Wadie turned toward her, and the smile grew gentle. "Sanity hasn't entirely disppeared from Heaven, Betha. Not even from the Rings. . . . Raul is a decent man; but more than that, he's not stupid. I told you his brother never won a chess game from me. In all the time I spent in the Rings, I won only two games from Raul. He may still have some surprises left."

Betha rubbed her arms. "All I know is that he intentionally infuriated the Demarchy to the point where they'll never be satisfied until they see us all in hell. Whatever he thinks he's doing, I don't like being his pawn."

The *Ranger* moved slowly out from Lansing. Betha watched it growing smaller below them, a world of elvish beauty, rising and falling in soft undulations beneath a transparent film of plastic spotted with milky patchwork. Trees reached upward toward the tent like sprays of lace, fragile fountains of leaves spilling over fields of ripening grain . . . and fields of dying grass. She saw the velvet green of parklands, still well watered . . . and the peeling mud of dried marshes. The people below moved in a dream ballet among airy minarets and pillared buildings of state, on the world that had once been the symbol of Heaven's splendid extravagance. The last world she would ever see. . . . She glanced at Clewell's still face, his closed eyes, where he drifted in his seat listening for the Demarchy's response. Afraid of the stillness, she looked away again, stroked Rusty's purring, clinging form while she tried to picture the other beloved faces already lost to her and the homeworld none of them would ever see again. There was no comfort now, no satisfaction, in this ultimate revenge that Heaven would inflict on itself in retribution for their deaths and her own. A terrible weariness settled over her, the futility of the last few weeks, the last four years.

"Betha . . ." Wadie kept his eyes on the screen. "I don't know how to save this ship. But I think I know how to save our lives. We can leave the *Ranger*, use the *Lansing 04* to take us down to Lansing. All Nakamore wants an end to is the ship, not our lives. If we use our suits we can all make it."

"No." Betha wrapped her arms across the aching muscles of her stomach. "I won't leave the *Ranger*. But yes, the rest of you, get into your suits and go. There's no reason for you to stay; at least save yourselves."

"What do you mean, you won't leave this ship?" Wadie pushed back from the screen, caught her chair arm. "It's just a ship, Betha; it doesn't control your life. You aren't chained to it."

She shook her head. "You still don't understand, do you? After all this time. This is *my* ship. I was part of its design, and part of its construction. Its crew were the people I loved; this journey meant everything to us, the future of our world. . . . Everything about it binds me to my people, my past, my home. I can't leave it. I don't want to lose everything, I don't want to live forever in the place where it happened. I don't want to live like that."

"Now who's indulging in the ultimate selfishness?"

Her mouth tightened. "It's not going to hurt anyone but me"—realizing, as she saw his face, that that wasn't true.

"Well, what about . . . what about Clewell?"

"What about me?" Clewell opened his eyes, irritably, at the communications board. "I have no intention of leaving the *Ranger* for that overgrown cinder down there."

"Damm it, you're just makin' her more stubborn. Why the hell don't you tell her she's wrong?"

"She's my wife, not my child. She has a right to make her own decision. And so do I. . . . I've lived too long already if I've lived to see this day. My body already knows the truth." He closed his eyes again. "Now let me do my job; monitoring the Demarchy is hard enough as it is at this distance."

"May it do us some good." Wadie pulled himself back to the panel, massaged the cramped muscles of his neck. "All right, then. . . . I'll stay too. I guess I've earned the right. I lost everythin' I ever valued because of this ship."

Betha froze her expression, willed emotion from her voice. "You won't blackmail me into changing my mind, Wadie."

He bowed solemnly. "Not my intent. Allow me the

privilege of making my own decision, since you expect me to accept yours. I'd rather die a martyr than a traitor."

She sighed, her nails digging into the palms of her hands. *Thank you.* "All right, then. So only two will be going to Lansing."

Bird Alyn raised her head from Shadow Jack's shoulder, drifting, cradled in his arms. "No. Betha, we're not goin'."

"Now, listen—"

"No," Shadow Jack said. "We did what we wanted to do for Lansing. But there's nothin' anybody can do for us. We'd rather be—together—now, for a little while, than be apart forever." He glanced at the doorway.

"I see." She nodded once, barely hearing her own voice. "Come here, then, both of you." They drifted forward obediently. Betha worked a golden band from one finger of each of her hands. Reaching out, she took their own left hands, one at a time, slipped a ring over a thin straight finger, a thin crooked one. She joined the hands to keep the rings from floating free. "By my authority as captain of this ship, I pronounce you husband and wife. . . . May your love be as deep as the darkness, as constant as the sun."

Their hands clung to her own for a moment; she felt Shadow Jack's trembling. She turned away, heard them leave the room. Clewell's eyes touched her face in a caress. "Pappy, get off the radio a minute. We've got to leave those people some hydrogen. . . ."

There were seventeen hundred seconds until encounter.

* * *

Three hundred kilometers away now, Lansing was a greenish, mottled crescent on the darkness. Far enough away, Betha hoped, to survive whatever fires must burn across Heaven. On all sides emptiness stretched, filling the light-years to the distant stars. And the *Ranger* had been built to bridge those distances, at speeds close to that of light itself. But it would never cross them again . . . it lay stranded like a beached cetoid on the desolate shores of Heaven, trapped by primitive ships with primitive weapons in the ultimate irony of defeat.

"Five hundred seconds," Wadie said. Rusty curled serenely in the crook of his arm and washed a protruding foot.

Betha lit her pipe, inhaled the familiar, soothing odor of the smoke. "That's when the first ship will pass; they're strung out at about one-hundred-second intervals. But it doesn't matter . . . we can't comply with MacWong's demand now."

Clewell chuckled suddenly, oblivious.

"God, Pappy, what in hell are you laughing at?"

He shook his head apologetically. "At the Demarchy reacting to Nakamore's speech—their righteous indignation at being named for what they are."

"Well, put it on," Wadie said, strangely eager. "I want to hear that."

A burst of static mixed with garbled speech filled the room. Clewell lowered the volume. "Sorry; even with enhancement, it takes some practice to make sense out of that."

Four hundred seconds.

He pulled off his ear jack. "My God, Betha, I think they're actually trying to take a vote . . . a vote on whether to let us go."

Betha pushed up out of her chair, caught herself on the panel edge with a gasp. "Pappy! Can't you clean up the transmission?"

"I'll try. MacWong's ships are close enough now; we may be in the tight beam from the Demarchy."

He put an image on the screen; Betha saw print, illegible through snow, recognized the format of a Demarchy general election. A band of golden yellow brightened at the bottom.

"It takes about five hundred seconds for a full tally."

"Five hundred! Christ." She felt Wadie move close, his sleeve brush her arm. "Pappy, raise MacWong's ship."

"I've tried. They're not talking."

She could almost see the numbers, almost see them change. And beside the static-clouded picture, the *Ranger*'s displays projected the track of three closing ships on a star-filled sky. Three ships that stood out like flares now, their torches extended ahead of their flight, decelerating at last. She searched their brilliance for a smaller track, a seed of blossoming destruction. *Give us time, MacWong*. . . . Clewell left his seat, moved slowly along the panel to her side; she took his arm. The digits on the chronometer narrowed like sand in an hourglass, eroding their lives. One hundred seconds until the first ship passed . . . sixty . . . fifty . . . She realized she had stopped breathing. "They're holding off! Forty seconds; that first ship can't fire on us now."

MacWong's face appeared below the tally. "Captain Torgussen." They saw the stress on his face and on the faces that ringed him in. "We're just now receivin' the results of a vote from the Demarchy. The majority accepts your aid to Lansing as evidence of your good will, Captain, and favors a modification of our mission. . . I hope you're listenin', Nakamore; you've just seen a demonstration of the real flexibility and strength of the people, the wisdom and fairness of the Demarchic system." He looked away, into the media cameras, and back.

"Captain Torgussen, the Demarchy will allow you

to depart—if you will assure us that the Demarchy will be the center for distributin' your aid when you return to Heaven." His eyes asked her to promise anything.

On the center of the screen Betha saw the second Demarchy ship fall past them.

Nakamore's image came onto the screen. "You know I can't accept that, MacWong." His voice was even, no longer reaching out to goad an entire people. "I don't demand that control go to the Harmony. But it's not goin' to you."

Betha froze, realizing that Nakamore might still let them go. A promise at knifepoint was no promise at all . . . and no solution. There had to be a way to reach both sides, or the next Morningside ship to come to Heaven would fall into the same deadly trap of greed. She heard someone come up behind her, turned to see Shadow Jack and Bird Alyn, peacefully hand in hand.

"What happened?" Bird Alyn brushed her soft floating hair back from her eyes and blinked at the screen.

Betha turned back to the screen, saw MacWong's pale eyes search her face for an answer. "It's going to be Lansing! Tell your people, MacWong, Nakamore. Those are Morningside's terms: our aid will be distributed through Lansing, the capital of the Heaven Belt. Neither of your governments will be shown favor, everyone will be treated equally."

They stared at her, unreal images; she saw Tiriki come alive, saw his mouth move soundlessly: ". . . a trick . . . want that ship destroyed . . ."

Wadie leaned past her. "Lansing's harmless, Lije! The Demarchy will accept it; you know they will."

MacWong moved back from the screen as Tiriki caught his shoulder; Betha read Tiriki's hatred. She looked at the computer plot. "That last ship will pass at only thirty kilometers; they can fire on us almost point-blank." She nodded at the screen. "If we don't see that ship pass by, we'll be stardust. . . ."

Behind her Shadow Jack said solemnly, "You mean we'll be dead."

MacWong broke away from Tiriki's grasp. She couldn't see his face, only that he faced the media's glaring eye and gave an order. . . .

Nakamore began to laugh. "Thank you, you son of chaos!"

A barely visible streak of palest violet lit the darkness on the screen before them for the length of a heartbeat, and was gone. The third ship had passed.

RANGER (LANSING SPACE) + 3.15 MEGASECONDS

"Crops may wither on the plain
Sun may parch us, rain turn wild—"

Clewell strapped himself into the navigator's seat, feeling new strength and satisfaction fill the hollow weariness of his limbs. He looked down at the running deflections on the panel, Shadow Jack holding Bird Alyn in his arms as she serenaded the long-suffering cat floating in midair across the room,

"Sharing brings us help for pain . . ."

The representatives of Heaven Belt. . . . Clewell smiled, seeing them many years older and wiser, many years into the future, returning again to Lansing. "I never thought I'd be saying it, but I may just live another sixty years."

Bird Alyn braced her feet against the wall to peer sideways at him. "I can't believe it's real, Pappy. How did it happen? How did it all come out like this?" Shadow Jack kissed her cheek; she giggled.

Wadie pushed away from the viewscreen, where Lansing lay before them on the now-empty night: a chrysalis waiting for rebirth into a new life cycle. "Nothin's gone right in Heaven Belt for two and a half billion seconds, Bird Alyn. There are a hundred million corpses out there and God knows how many people who've gone through living hell. . . ." Bird

Alyn's smile faltered; Shadow Jack held her tighter, the past darkened their eyes.

Wadie shook his head. "We must have paid for our mistake by now, a thousand times over. It's about time we had some good luck, dammit! It's about time."

Their faces eased. Clewell saw Betha look up from the panel, covering other memories, other sorrows. "Yes, it is. Pappy"—her voice was even—"everything's secured, the sky is empty. Start charting our course; it's time to go home." Wadie moved back to her side; Clewell saw his hand lift, hesitate, and drift away, still uncertain. He had been beside her for days: helping, learning . . . watching Betha Torgussen with an intentness that had nothing to do with starship technology. The man who would be a hero someday when their ship returned, MacWong had said; but who for now was still a traitor . . . and the only trade consultant who would satisfy both the Demarchy and the Rings. A good man, Clewell thought; the right man. Like another good man who had loved his wife and been his friend.

Clewell felt Betha's eyes touch him once more, as blue as field flowers, still shadowed by memory and pain. *Time heals all things* . . . and they would have the time they needed now. She changed the image on the screen. It showed him numberless stars; and one among the millions—shrunken, red, and constant—that would guide them home.

Laughter floated out of the room and down the stairwell as Bird Alyn and Shadow Jack, unknowing and unconcerned, put the past behind them forever.

Rusty settled onto his shoulders, purring in soft harmony with the memory of song:

Sharing brings us help for pain,
For nothing's easy, oh my child.

He saw the faces of his other children, who he hoped would live to see the better world that had cost so much and been so long in coming. "Rusty," he said quietly, "it's about time."

About the Author

JOAN D. VINGE has had stories published in *Analog, Orbit, Isaac Asimov's SF Magazine*, and various anthologies, including *The Crystal Ship* (title novella) and *Millennial Women*. Two of her novellas have been published as a book entitled *Fireship*.

Joan has a degree in anthropology, which she feels is very similar to science fiction in many ways because both fields give you an opportunity to view human relationships from a fresh and revealing perspective. She's worked, among other things, as a salvage archeologist, enjoys horseback riding and needlecrafts, and is married to Vernor Vinge, who also writes science fiction.